A Curious Host

A Curious Host

NANETTE L AVERY

This is a work of fiction. Names, characters, places, and incidents, are the products of the author's imagination or are used fictitiously. Any resemblance to actual events, locales, or persons, living or dead, is entirely coincidental.

ISBN: 1523766557
ISBN 13: 9781523766550
Library of Congress Control Number: 2016901961
CreateSpace Independent Publishing Platform
North Charleston, South Carolina

This book is dedicated to
Louise and Kathy
(and… to all those who like dogs and don't mind what they think of us)

———

Prologue

The salesman had a grin as long as the river, and when he spoke it flooded the room with chatter and idle talk about this or that, but mostly about the cutlery he was selling. It was the yellow dog that first treated him kindly when he came into the plain town, a sprawling sea of opportunity that was marked ready for him to cast his pitch. The dog was walking aimlessly along the sidewalk and stopped when the man carrying his rather large valise of knives, individually wrapped in cloth, also stopped before crossing the street. He wouldn't have made much notice except that the dog seemed genuinely interested in him, more than most of the folks he had tried to sell to. So, he decided to share a meal with the dog and with very little coaxing they sat together at the bus bench and divided a cheese sandwich, which the kindly man had in his bag. It was neatly cut into evenly quartered pieces, having used one of his paring knives to slice the bread.

The yellow dog ate its portion in two gulps without waiting for the man to finish his. Grateful as the animal was, it thanked the man the best it knew how, with a wet lick across his cheek, whereupon it scampered away leaving the lonely salesman with the only positive impression of his visit.

How difficult and friendless life can be for the traveling salesman; but for this stranger it was even more tragic; barely had he resumed his travels when several days after this encounter, he was found quite dead in his motel room fifty miles away and quite alone.

One

THE TOWN

If ever it was said that life was dull it would have been by the impatient dreamers. For even those of us who have not traveled the world have only to look outside our thresholds to witness a myriad of activities. Early, before the sun rises and the changing of light, we will find the newspaper delivery person; for it is his or her job to ensure the news is neatly rolled, rubber-banded, and then strategically tossed by whatever means chosen at the home of the subscriber. It is a lonesome job for the streets are generally quiet; seldom is there a person talking for the night is struggling to wake and except for an intermittent thud of the paper striking a lawn or falling into a bush that may interrupt what sleepers would consider tranquility, it is still the hour before haste begins.

In the quietest part of the day, right after the rain, when the potholes fill with water and cracks form tributaries to carry the run-off into the ditches; that's when there is a cleansing. The asphalt patched like an old tire and the buckled sidewalk hold together fine enough for tufts of grass, but make a poor path for the walker. It's a tired neighborhood, tired from having to take the blame for all the woes, tired that the weeds creep into all spaces that aren't cemented over, tired of fences, just damn tired.

The dog sleeps under the brush, the scrubs, the parked cars, and before the sun and after the rain. It drifts into morning, eats its breakfast in the alley where the dented tin cans lean against one another, and where the lazy good-for-nothing busboy, cause that's what he is called by the owner, the good-for-nothing busboy, never tends to the cans in a righteous way. There are always potato peelings or griddle-grease stuck to the lids that are easily toppled off, and the dog licks them with his greedy tongue until there is no more. Then he knocks them over, and with his paw pushes aside the vegetable scraps and scarfs up the chicken bones and grizzle. It likes the good-for-nothing busboy, even though they have never met. And the boy hates the dog, even though they have never met because he always gets a slap on the back of his head and then cleans up the mess.

It once had a fine coat, smooth and yellow and its teeth were clean for it was taken good care of and it ate well, but not anymore; and the dog doesn't really care because he knows where to get breakfast.

———

There is a strange odor in the air, strange because it is unnatural; a putrid kind of stink that hovers low and is carried by the wind until the rain flushes it into the gutters, and it flows and swirls till it reaches the faraway river; the enormous river that floods when there is too much rain. The banks swell and are pummeled by the brutish waters; a one-sided fight that was designed to drag and drown. Watermarks stained the rotting wood pilings and week after week they would rise, rise an inch higher and the government man in the government issued truck would drive over to examine the levels, and then one day he didn't return. The yellow dog was at the top of the hill when the waters breached the levee. He hid under the bus bench and even though the rain dripped through the wooden slats, he just stayed there all balled-up. He couldn't see the river but he could hear it, and it careened with the fury of a freight train and grabbed up everything in its way. It uprooted trees, tossed over cars, flattened fences, and broke down doors. The yellow dog hid all day and all night at the top of the hill, and though it could hear voices calling in the blackness, chilled voices of men and women, it never left its place. It wasn't sure if it heard its name, but when the rain was over and the sun came up, it shook off the mud and trundled back down the hill.

And so when misery comes to a plain town, no one seems to take too much notice recounting the whereabouts of a dog. Some believe that one dog is the same as the next. When one goes missing it hardly seems worth the trouble looking for it. Maybe that's why it seemed so peculiar, the way the gray man kept going on about the dog. Trolling up and down the street, kicking up mud and muttering how he'd kill that ungrateful mongrel when he finally caught up with it. For a whole week the gray man patrolled the neighborhoods, even posted a copy of the dog's picture with a reward of ten dollars for its return. A few folks came round his shanty of a house, with its moth bitten curtains and crooked porch; a few tried to say that they had some clues. The drunkard, Gil Adler, claimed to have seen the dog and for a half-pint of Old Crow he'd take him to where the mutt was last seen, but the gray man's wickedness only got the best of him, and he tossed the damn fool out on his ass right into the gully by the side of the dirt road. He was strong and most men didn't like to cross him and even though he worked as a clerk at the post office and had enough money to keep his home fixed-up fine, he didn't; the only thing that looked good was the dog...but now it was gone.

Two

THE PLAN

The dog hated to be confined and like most canine its disposition changed as defiantly as a cold wind. By nature the animal was docile, obedient to sit and stay if commanded, permitted its coat to be groomed, and its mouth and teeth to be examined. But once it thought that there was chance of being chained or penned, it no longer prescribed to such submissive behaviors. The dog owned a free spirit and if need be would uproot a tree before settling under it with a chain attached to its collar. It had a knack for avoiding such things, and as such there were some who believed that it may even be possessed.

The Rosewater children once cornered him in the alley across from the laundromat, and though it was a rather stupid thing to do, no harm came to any of the insipid little beings. But the tale they spun about how it came leaping over their heads when they approached with a good strong rope remains a legend around the schoolyard.

The heat was especially hostile that July afternoon, and the dog was loitering about town letting its nose lead it to no good, like it often seemed to do; when the three Rosewaters: Jackson, Grant, and James; all named for Presidents, were walking back from the matinee for they had all proclaimed it was too hot to play outdoors, when they noticed the dog. It was too busy to pay much attention to them for its head dragged along the road like a duster. And though it was paying mind to no one, the three imps found a rather amusing pastime… sneaking up behind and daring each other to grab the tail that was flickering feverishly. The youngest one, Jackson, was not the smallest in stature; he was a brute of a seven-year-old and seemed to take the greatest delight in this new found game. He would ever-so-quietly skip along, bend forward, and tap lightly on the tail as though it were a flexible antenna. The front of the dog did not seem to mind what the back was doing and with each tap the children found that they could influence its path as though it were being moved along by remote control. This playful manipulation went on for some time, until the dog, unbeknownst to its brain, was led into an alley.

Grant, who had been too lazy to look for his belt that morning when dressing, now untied the rope he had used instead and demonstrated that with a simple noose the three of them could easily lasso the dog and claim it as their captive. He slid the makeshift belt off from around his waist and grinned eagerly as the dog trotted his way into the alley. With legs spread apart the boys made a semi-circle, cornering the unassuming animal. All three danced in place and dared one another to plant the rope around its neck, but none had the nerve for the canine had wedged itself behind a dumpster and remained quite content as it scavenged for anything edible.

"It already got a collar," Grant whispered. "Let's just call it over and we can tie the rope like a leash." A splendid idea had been announced, but when taunts of "Here dog, here boy," were echoed, the scrounger lifted its head and peered out from round the green dumpster without much interest and went back to its garbage.

Again the small voices summoned the hound, but this time with the help of a bargaining chip; for Jackson had dug into his pocket and retrieved a half-eaten piece of bread. Dangling it, he edged closer, wagging the bait as one wiggles a worm at the end of the fishing line. "Here you go boy, a nice piece of ..." but before the words were issued from his lips the dog had emerged from behind and snapped up the bread with the ferocity of a barracuda!

"Shit, he nearly took my finger!" screamed the boy and ran back to the other two who found the entire incident amusing. "I ain't going back over there, he bites!" exclaimed the victim displaying his hand now splattered with the dog's saliva. Both brothers leaned forward and examined the complainer's finger with an obligatory inspection.

"Hell, he doesn't bite! What did you think he would do?" announced James, the eldest but not necessarily the smartest. "Come on, we'll just go round and when we get close we can grab him."

"Grab him?" asked Jackson, now skeptical of this approach.

"Yes, smartass, grab him!"

And by way of three separate perspectives under one plan of attack, they slinked towards the opening. No sooner had the trio begun to slither into the small space did the dog turn with such a vicious snarl that the putrid stink from its breath created an even more alarming scene as saliva splattered everywhere.

"Run, run!" panicked Grant, "run for your life, it's gonna to kill us!" A unanimous shriek of fear was sounded as the three menaces squealed with horror. But rather than attacking, the dog crouched close to the ground and with impeccable agility sprung over the three boys and raced away, all-the-while still hanging on to what looked like the carcass of a mouse.

For this reason, the legend had begun; the face-to-face experience with an irritated and quite athletic dog had become synonymous with the Rosewater boys' repertoire of phantasmagoria. The yellow dog had made its place in the history of the plain town.

Three

THE FIGHT

Jen was one of four sisters. She was the third in line, each being not much more than a year apart. They were all drunks at an early age which was not a surprise being as their mother was a drunk. As for her father, he could have been any one of a collection of men, but she never found out and never really seemed to care. Jen lived in a tidy house with her cousin, JJ, an aloof woman with artistic hands and a plow. One of the only mule-drawn plows in the county sat marooned in the front yard. During the summer sunflowers grew up between the handles and dandelions found their way along the frame of the mainshare. JJ claimed the antique belonged to their great-grandmother, but this too could have been a bold lie since no one ever challenged the story. She was too indifferent and too ornery and no one in the plain town really gave a damn anyway. Had JJ been a teenager in the '20s she would have been a flapper. Her confidence typified all that was independent, the way she carried herself and her self-assurance convinced those around her that she was not a woman to be reckoned with. She ate at off-hours and napped when she was tired, regardless of the time of day. Though a woman of large stature, she conveyed the impression that she had been chiseled from marble.

The dog liked JJ because she always would feed it bones. Whenever she cooked chicken, at least twice a week, she would set out the discarded bones and skin for the scavenging animals. If the dog was lucky it would get there before the possums or raccoons. They were dusk hunters, foragers that trespassed when others came in for the night; except for the dog that liked to wander. JJ didn't mind the dog, but she and its owner were forever at odds.

———

Gil Adler wasn't always a drunk, and he wasn't always a bum, but he was always pitiful. He came from a long line of liars on his father's side, and his mother's side were mostly zealots and gamblers. His line of ancestry followed a notorious trail of trouble, bad luck, and a heap of rottenness. Such was the plight of each Adler.

———

It rained hard Saturday afternoon; it beat against the window of the *Sitting Pretty Lounge* and shellacked the pane so furiously that it managed to clean the soot right off the old sills. It was just one of many Saturdays that JJ whipped her opponents in 5-Card Draw, and this afternoon it was her turn again. She liked to win and liked even more to flaunt it. She was notorious for being a poor winner, blowing cigar smoke into little ringlets as her distended cheeks puffed in and out like a goldfish. Her impatient hands would swoop forward and shovel the winning chips towards her; raking them in as though they were a pile of autumn leaves. Puffing and grunting with delight; it was an especially distasteful scene. And had the gray-haired man not have mentioned it, then just maybe there would not have been the fight. But no woman, no matter how coarse she may behave, likes to be reminded of such.

"You sure are acting ugly." He picked up his beer and let it flow down his throat, and as he returned the empty glass to the table, it settled with a thud. A foamy moustache frothed over his upper lip and before it could drip, he wiped his mouth with the sleeve of his jacket. His eyes met hers, and they were silent. She cocked her head and pursed her lips together as though she were going to say something, but a defiant laugh erupted instead; she leaned into the table and pulled the pile towards her so it now was teetering at the edge with her large bosoms blocking any chips from slipping down onto her lap. She exposed little weakness, and in her illusory way always arranged to make her opponent appear foolish or weak.

Gil Adler, half-perched on a stool, was watching. Slumped against the bar, his head rolled back and forth on his thin neck as he tipped up and back on the seat, peering over to get a glimpse of the cards. "You ain't so ugly, JJ," he professed. He squeezed his lids tightly together and with his thumb and index finger brought the small slot he had formed up to his eye and peered at her through the tiny opening. His words slurred as he jested again, "Well, maybe justa' little."

She returned a deadpan glare and her mouth quivered; the same kind of quiver that vibrates the kettle's lid just before releasing its impatient whistle. On nearly all occasions JJ's most envied trait was maintaining an unruffled composure during those very moments when her opponents were having difficulty keeping their tempers in check. But today she misplaced her balance. An exaggerated exhale spewed from her nostrils, and she picked up her half-lit cigar from the tin ashtray and inhaled. The tip reignited and the woman sucked hard.

The gray man surveyed the table and pushed himself away. A blend of stale smoke shimmied up and over him. It stung his eyes and they were bloodshot from the beer and tobacco and disgust. He blinked and mumbled, "Damn ugly." She looked up, but this time he knew that he might have provoked her. It felt good knowing that she had feelings too. The gray man smirked, put his hands in his pockets and tipped back on his heels.

The incensed woman puffed harder and the stub of the cigar came alive as a trail of ash grew longer and longer until it dropped onto the table and smoldered. Then, it went out. "Teddy, another Ballantine." Her voice canvassed the room with a commanding gruffness. "And get another one for my friend," she added and flicked her hand towards his chair. Her nails were long and polished and well-manicured.

"No, none for me," he said.

However, JJ was not used to being turned down and found herself intrigued by this challenge. "Come on, you look like you could use another. It's on me!" But like JJ, the man was not one to compromise and shook his gray head with a solemn "no". The customers were an unruly mix of single men and women, and they chattered loudly, one-to-the-other, infusing periodic outbreaks of high-pitched laughter. The irritated woman slung herself forward, upsetting the pile of chips that were scattered loosely on the table. "Why not?" she retorted smartly; her breath so thick that it carried the words towards the man. "Don't tell me you're a poor loser?"

He rubbed his stubbled chin and as he crafted an answer the drunk stumbled towards the conversation and lumbered up to his side. "Ugly, you said she was ugly," the fool exclaimed in an over-exaggerated whisper. Then he staggered round the table and propped his foot up on the chair rung and leaned into the woman's ear. "Said you were ugly," and when he spoke spittle shot out of his mouth.

And so this is how on the rainy afternoon the fight broke out. It wasn't a long fight, but just long enough for the two men to realize that it wasn't the polite thing to do, call a lady ugly. With less than a moment's notice the friction of these words suddenly ignited like the rubbing together of two sticks. The character of the woman dominated the room as she sent Gil Adler to the ground with the stool he was relying on to keep him steady and swung it with a mighty force towards the gray man. Fortuitous that it had been made with inferior wood, it cracked into several pieces, all of which made the target look as though he had been thrown under a grand pile of kindling when he dropped to the floor. She stood over him, her arms crossed and her head bowed low. "I'll show you ugly!"

All eyes had converged on the back of the room for it was a bright enough bit of entertainment on such a dreary day to get their attention. JJ picked up her winnings and tossed several bills onto the table. She walked past the gray man and stepped over any dignity he may have hoped to recover. The haze of tobacco smoke and the cavorting of laughter filled in the gaps of the day as he got up and limped past the bartender and back into the somber afternoon.

For several more hours the rain fell and the bartender swept up the broken stool and stood the legs up against the corner of the room, except for one that he placed behind the bar. And before twilight confiscated the end of the day he took up his broom again, prodding beneath the table for Gil Adler to get on home.

Four

J en, not the prettiest but the most ambitious of her sisters, and the mother had all lived together in disharmony, for each was always suspicious of the other. Although they had nothing to base such claims upon, the older they grew the greater their dislike for one another fermented. The days in the small house were short but the nights were long with drink. And as the sun shone into the mud-stained windows and abandoned its yellow streaks across the plastic covered couch, there was not a clear head to be found.

The mother was an overly friendly woman who never turned down an opportunity to invite a willing guest to Sunday dinner; and having four daughters, she made it her business not to do the cooking but the entertaining. The table would be set with a vase of store-bought gladiolas, plastic salt and pepper shakers, and a white or blue tablecloth. In the summers the open windows attracted listeners and flies, and if you were walking past you could hear the clanging of forks against the plates. The corn-on-the cob was slippery with chicken grease and butter, and they licked their fingers until it was time for pie. After dinner the mother would retire to the backyard with a bottle of whiskey or rye or whatever the Sunday guest may have brought. When there was nothing else to be shared and the sky was no longer black but pleats of gray, she would come in to bed.

It's an ordinary place, the house; a blend of useable and useless items scattered here and there, some stashed on shelves, others stowed beneath furniture. Several bowls of used corks lining the counter, a stack of outdated magazines wedged into the corner, and a tray of mismatched utensils nested in the drawer; any or all of these items may later be of use and therefore deemed a necessary provision in the kitchen. There was the back closet that no one entered. It was filled with papers, important papers that could not be thrown away. So it remained sealed, for to open it would mean inviting into the rest of the house whatever vermin had taken up residence between the clutter and dust and musty boxes. Leaning up along the inside wall of the garage was a yellowing bedspring and a mattress that had lost all its energy. Paint cans with unreadable labels and dented lids, half-used turpentine, and stiff brushes possessed a rotting shelf, while above it a row of jars remained ready for use; glass jars in all sizes pushed up against the wall, front to back. It was estimated that there were at least 189, but no one bothered to count. In the bottom of the oldest jars, the carcasses of summer moths and bluebottle flies lay smothered in blankets of dust, and as though attached by gossamer threads, cobwebs interlaced between the clutter like crisscrossing high-wires for creeping insects.

One evening a thought crept up like a crocus flower in the spring. It bloomed overnight and when it blossomed the next morning, Jen moved out.

———

A house, if it is small, may be referred to as cozy, but after cousin Jen moved into the spare room, it was snug. The younger woman had arrived in good spirits with all intentions of paying her share of the expenses. Having a bit of savings in the bank and the prospects of getting a secretarial job upon completion of her mail-order courses, she promised not to be a burden. However, in spite of her private concerns, JJ welcomed her cousin not as a house guest but as a member of the family. And so, the cottage that had been devoid of laughter ever since her husband's untimely disaster no longer was just a house, but rather a home.

———

The oversized-swing rocked back and forth with just enough momentum to keep it going forever. From the porch Jen could watch everyone and anything that passed by. During the late afternoons when the sun settled down, hanging over the horizon as if on a clothesline, when the sky shifted from pale blue to pale gray, she would begin her daily wait for JJ to come home from work. There was something unfair about her cousin being just a bookkeeper at the survey office, for she knew more about building roads than the men in the field. But how much knowledge a woman had was not of importance, and she kept her ideas to herself behind the office desk while revealing her cunning side at the card table.

This was the hour of day children would be called in to wash up for supper and cars and trucks were parked any-which-way. It was the hour of day when everyone in the plain town seemed to be on the same path, all led by their innate instincts like homing pigeons. JJ was easy to identify for she walked with a brisk gait. She strutted as though she owned the world, and Jen liked that. The impatient woman would shade her hand over her brow, even though there was no sun to block, and when the stately woman came into view she would wave her hand towards the house as though she were at a pit stop guiding her in. Then she would sit down on the swing and they would rock, and giggle, and pour several glasses of bourbon until the fireflies came out and they knew it was time for supper.

Occasionally, during the day, the dog would traipse down the road and Jen would call it over; and it would sit under the shade of the crooked porch roof and let her stroke its yellow head. She liked to pet him because he was soft, and his fur reminded her of a dog she once owned when she was little. But that was a long time ago.

It was unreasonable having to share a pet, especially when you believed it was a birthday present. Honey was a small and velvet-eared cocker spaniel. It was brought into the house right after Uncle Jerry left, and while it seemed curious that the mother replaced the man with a dog, the timing was right and she professed that a dog was easier to train. Even though it didn't arrive exactly on her birthday, Jen's was the closest in line of the sisters, and so the puppy was proclaimed hers under the unanimous moans of, "It's not fair!" Honey seemed like the most obvious name being as its color was identical to the sticky syrup, and although the youngest sister made the suggestion to call it Jerry, this idea was quickly vetoed by the mother. She said she didn't want any more reminders, even if he was a dog.

Never had the plain town seen such a fancy little dog, and though it did not like to be hooked to a leash, the sisters took turns clipping it on and taking it outside. But the little beast had a nasty habit of sitting instead of walking and though they flattered it with their most endearing voices and small dove-like cooing, it simply would not abide. Finally after days of trying, they concocted a scheme. One would walk in front and entice him with a piece of meat, a sort of bait-like approach. Surely, they believed, this would get the little vixen to move on its own. And so the plan was set into motion; with just a small flaw; the only meat they found in the refrigerator was an uncut roll of salami.

The idea seemed like it would work, but to their disappointment the only thing the four managed to do was feed the little dog an entire salami, at which point it becoming quite full and chose to lay in the sun without any intention of moving. And so, he was slid across the yard with each sister taking a turn, until finally reaching the house where he was carried inside and promptly threw-up his bribe all over the carpet. Needless to say, Honey's days were numbered and the small companion lasted just a little longer than Jerry. "What good is a dog that won't listen? I might as well as kept, Jerry," the mother announced. "At least he could drive."

———

It took almost a week of sunshine for the plain town to dry out. The gullies along the sides of the roads that had been gushing with water during the storms now displayed telltale signs of its wrath. They were littered with flat stones, bark-colored leaves, and debris the rain had absconded with and now discarded for the scavengers to pick through. What was once slathered in mud was now encased in a shell of hardened clay, and it had stuck to anything it could. Toppled tree limbs and branches blocked driveways, streets, and paths that were seldom taken. Yet, folks were used to the mess and went about their business picking up lawn chairs and replanting displaced shrubs, and though things were getting back to normal for most, the yellow dog had not returned home. The gray man continued to set out its food in a large plastic bowl. But by the following morning most of it had been eaten by the marauding raccoons that liked to topple it over and single out the larger pieces as if they were choosing ripe tomatoes in the market. However, it was the black grackles that were far less fastidious, stalking the dog's dish from a good 20 feet away until they felt it was safe, and then with ferocity they would dive down, snatch a kibble of food, swallow it whole, and greedily come back for more.

Five

We come into the world already named and for the most part much consideration had been taken in arranging its choice. Yet despite all the thought and deliberation under which it was conceived and finalized, a name does not really belong to us unless we allow it to become our calling card.

———

When Pearl came into the world she was Mary and for sixteen years she answered to what she believed to be a most ordinary name, a moniker which she had inherited from an aunt she had never met. Her connection to the dead woman had been rooted only by their sharing of a first name and though she felt no bond, no loving connection, she was a living reminder of the deceased and was referred to as Little Mary. But with time's unsupervised passing of years, she learned to dislike the woman, an aunt that represented everything she was not; a conventional prude whose reputation was synonymous with prohibition. To that end, Little Mary conspired to rid herself of the woman's subliminal hold.

Living on an income of time, the decision to change her name and the color of her hair came simultaneously. In only a few hours her features were transformed and for the next twenty years, every month or so, she would go into the bathroom and come out a fresh shade of copper. It got so that she believed she must have been a red-head in another life, and as a fair-haired woman declared the world was as fragile as an oyster bed and she was its "Pearl".

Pearl was a dreamer and her desires were greater than the plain town. She fanaticized being sketched in an artist's notebook, to be a favorite subject created out of bohemian energy. He would arrive on foot, a hitchhiker with no more ambitions than beyond the next form, the next image, the next drawing, the next town. He would sit at the corner table, his back leaning against the yellowing wall with a foot up and pad braced against his knee, and he would watch her as she sallied about. As the day grew she would try to look at the drawing, but he would brush his hand over it with modest disclosure. Then, when her shift was over he would retreat back into the night with her image.

————

The truckers looked forward to seeing Pearl when they stopped just outside the plain town for a cup of coffee and a meatloaf sandwich. Her whole world was the diner and she courted good times by flirting and teasing. No deep or sinister motives could have given her reason to be friendly. It was an instinct of self-preservation and a touch of loneliness that were roused by their overtures. Her laugh was genuine and hearty, which profited her with a goodly number of generous tips. The ebb and flow in her moods were none the more different than others who had used up nearly all of their time working; unmoved, desirous, willful, coy, she experimented with them all.

She was to the diner what nightclubs are to big cities. She greeted each customer like a good morning stretch and delighted in taking strangers into her confidence. They came in to eat at all hours of the day, but no matter how crowded no one ever complained that the food was served cold. The platters sat unattended for only a few moments because when Connie tapped the bell, its ring never got lost in the hum of conversations. With a waitress's gait she could make her way to the counter, line her forearm with the clunky dinner plates, and balance them without a quiver as she sashayed back to the table. The compliments were flirtatious, the patrons attentive, and even though her feet hurt at the end of every shift she didn't mind. The diner made the plain town seem not so plain. Every now and again a picture postcard from some far off place arrived and she'd tack it up on the wall above the stack of menus, which often stuck one-to-another in their plastic coverings. And when the card was addressed to "Red", she knew there was a story to be heard when the sender stopped back in.

Pearl and Connie were sparring partners, scrapping like a pair of alley cats; yet even while airing their differences it was easy to recognize they were compatible. She was as restless as the ocean, and when the day held on too tight, he would remind her that he was but a simple rowboat following in her wake.

There was a time when the diner's reputation rested solely on its good food and generous portions; an honest place to eat when you don't feel like cooking. It promised all the makings of a homemade meal without the fuss. But when the highway extension was added, its popularity surpassed all expectations. The diner's reputation heightened not because of if its dependable menu or good service. It was on account of its unintentional location.

Now, this highway hadn't been built without controversy and at the initial mention of the project a great wall of resistance was erected. It was immediately forged with skepticism and distrust, demonstrating to those in favor that they would need a scheme to break down the barrier of opposition. Town Hall meetings offering explanations of its glossy benefits shined a positive spin, and while appearing as a patriotic duty to give in without discourse, it was not universally popular. Many residents didn't see the giving up of land in quite the same light. Tempers flared, protests were staged, but it wasn't long before the lawyers came up with a seemingly fitting arrangement. Prices several percent higher than market value were finally agreed upon as money was exchanged for surrendered property that had long been over-farmed and over-tired like the people who tilled it. Those that sold were remunerated to their liking, but as in all eminent domain stories not all land was given up willingly or agreeably without a final battle. Though as hard as they tried, the big road was their ultimate providence and as always, so it seems, the politicians got their way.

The plain town hadn't seen many changes, but when the country road was widened to four lanes and the paving machines finally rumbled away it meant more trucker business. The diner's new marquee courted the hungry and tired with its blinking lights; touting itself as one of the last stops for a home-style meal and clean restroom before the eighty-mile stretch. And as business increased it was deemed necessary to hire more help for the evening shift. Jessie, a young drifter who fit the black and white uniform well enough to get an extra tip was hired. As for Pearl, as long as it wasn't another redhead, the extra help suited her just fine.

––––––

The gray man pouted before the television. He nursed his head with a limp icepack in need of refilling, but seeing as he had forgotten to fill the ice trays there were no more frozen cubes. He looked at his watch and wondered how long it would take for the water to harden; at last check a thin brittle skin had formed, but he poked too hard and it cracked.

"Damn ugly woman," he bemoaned and shifted uncomfortably in his easy-chair. The plaid cushion was wearing thin where he sat. He eyed the dog's blanket next to the chair and his thoughts wandered away from the commercial. It was almost a week since the big rain. He tossed the limp icepack onto the coffee table, stood up, and lumbered over to the window. He pulled the curtain aside and stared into the darkness. The windowpane had fogged over with the dampness of the night air, and he wiped it dry with his shirttail. The streetlight dappled the road without much energy. He glanced up at the lit windows of the house across the street. "Damn dog," he muttered and turned into the kitchen to check the ice trays.

––––––

When a girl turns seventeen, an age which she is neither old enough to buy a beer or old enough to cast a vote, one of two things will occur. She may muddle her way through the labyrinth of life's adventures with youthful optimism, or she will fail miserably due to irrevocably poor choices.

Jessie tossed the pillow onto the front seat and opened the back door. An uncomfortable rush of cold air entered her meager domain, and she drew back into the car. However, it was her need for cash that proved tougher than the harsh weather, and it pushed her out into the parking lot. She leaned against the door and stretched, pulled her watch out of her pocket and checked the time. The air stung and she clasped her cold hands together and blew between them. The stars were swarming and there was a sliver of the moon stalking behind a cloud. She pulled her collar up over her neck and hurried towards the diner. A stiff square man held the door open as she approached.

"Thanks, thanks a lot!" Her gratitude was lost between winded gasps and she slid by him before he could acknowledge.

But he was already distracted by three burly drivers who greeted him with a boisterous, "Over here!" A stale smell hovered around the men emanating from a trail of beer that lingered after each one spoke, but following a few cups of coffee it would be exchanged for a more admissible breath and then they could be on their way.

It was dinnertime; the diner was full except for a few empty stools at the counter. Connie was tapping the bell like he was calling a bellhop as Jessie scooted past the counter-window into the back hallway. Above the portal was tacked a crudely painted sign, "restrooms".

"Good you're here, Jill." The cook offered a forced smile over his shoulder with a gesture of "hurry it up".

The younger waitress slung her jacket on a peg and exchanged it for a starched apron. It covered her loosely, and she tied the sash until it was snug around her narrow waist. She pushed open the bathroom door and closed it firmly behind her, irritated as to when he was going to remember her name correctly. The water ran cold into the basin. She cupped her hands and splashed water on her face. She shivered like a wet dog and turned the handle marked "hot", but it spewed only air. She tugged on the cloth hanging from the towel dispenser; however, adding to her frustration the next section rolled round to a soggy length of used linen. "Crap!" She dried her face on her apron. The feeling of disgust and boredom re-erupted. She could hear a voice outside the bathroom. Her purse hung over her shoulder like a limp animal and dangled freely, hitting the sink as she twisted round.

"Comin' out soon?" The tone was sarcastic and irritated.

"Be right there." She rolled her eyes back into her head. And though she wasn't too good at most things, she was very good at that. She rummaged through her bag and picked out several bobby pins; pulled back her hair, curled it around behind her head, and pushed the pins through. She wiped the sleepers from her eyes and doubted anyone would notice the run in her stocking. But it didn't matter much. She opened the door and looked across the diner and out through the window. The moon was up and it shined more brightly than she had seen in a while. It cast a silver sheen over the parking lot and glinted across the hoods of the trucks like rocks skipping across a lake. They appeared much more dazzling under the moonbeams and for a second she was filled with a tinge of envy. She looked back around the room until she found a target. Attached to her curiosity was a man seated at the end of the counter. "The blue one's driver," she smiled to herself and stepped forward with a renewed sense of promise.

Six

The mood of the plain town is like a string of pearls, some days more lustrous than others. The talking, the gossiping, the haggling, and the fighting roam ghostlike through every household emancipating the will of its residents. It is the fodder that upholds traditions and keeps its customs in check.

———

Most of the houses in the plain town were built of wood construction and raised-up on blocks with a crawlspace shared by small woodland creatures and neighborhood kids playing hide-and-seek. They line the dirt roads, all of a similar design, pitched roofs, open front porches, and gravel walkways leading up from the street to sets of planked steps. They housed generations and harbored both their hardships and celebrations, and through war and renewal the folks raised their families, planted their gardens, and buried their dead. And no matter what was going on outside their small world, the plain town grew in population. But it was the flood of '48 that defined the stronger passion between man and nature. This was the storm that triumphed, and it mercilessly took out most of the homes at the bottom of the hill. Had residents not been offered low interest loans to fix their houses, there might not be the plain town we have today. Some folks accepted the credit and replaced the water-soaked wood with aluminum siding, and then there were others that were distrustful of the bank, the new method of repair, or both, and resolved to patch the ruined wood with hewed lumber. Although it seemed like a good solution at the time, this proved to be erroneous for the wood used had been soaking in river water, unscrupulously dried and resold as new.

But of all the homes in the plain town it was the house on the very top of the hill that was the most coveted. The house on the top of the hill is white as freshly fallen snow and in the winter when the grass lies dormant beneath an icy cap, it resembles a small imperfection against the gray sky like a dove in a birch tree. Matthew Kamer and his wife, Matilda, bought it from the Louis family after the great flood. And though it had miraculously withstood much wind damage, save a half-dozen shingles that slid off the gable, it was in need of repair and a good coat of paint. The elder Louis was the last living relative to have inherited the house and with no heirs; when the mortgage came due, he decided to sell. It isn't a very large house, but it has plenty of land that rolls and tumbles down around it and akin to the crown of a wedding cake, it sits quite contently.

In the springtime the road leading up to the hilltop is lined with lily of the valley, and though the weeds once flourished with pompous airs, they have since surrendered as if having been trained to keep away. In the summer the grass is thick and green from the rains, and the lily of the valley makes way for the aster with their "don't care attitude" that they never get any respite from the heat. "The blessed Kamer land" is what the pious folks call the house on the hill with its white façade and colorless framed windows. Matthew Kamer is a quiet man, a biologist by profession, who spends most spring and summer days outdoors, but when the colder months grow tiresome he rarely ventures to town. For several years he and his wife lived contently, but now he is alone. And so it is that most folks in the plain town keep to themselves. When Mrs. Kamer died there were the usual questions of how, the usual gossip, but with the hushes and whispers there was also respect for the elderly couple, and truthfully no one felt her departure was really more insidious than the normal progression of life.

There trailed a snake-like procession of mourners behind the black hearse as the long car crept slowly down the road leading from the house on the hill carrying a white coffin made of birch. It was a beautiful box, lined in pale blue silk, and she was as stately a woman as anyone could ever remember. Her snowy curls capped her round head, and her face was light and soft except for the red lipstick that Dr. Kamer could not ever remember her wearing before. "Mattie looks just like the queen I married," he remarked and kissed her forehead the same way he always did before she went to bed.

And had a bird been peering down, this unified movement heading to the church must have looked like a line of insects marching along the road, for those in attendance wore the customary black with Dr. Kamer leading the troop wearing the tuxedo he had been married in. The wind was brisk in the cloudless sky, and unlike the others he was hatless. Like puffs of flax his thick hair glistened in the sunlight, a curious contrast to the somber moment. When the service was over the cortege marched back up the hill to the house where Mrs. Kamer was then laid to rest many yards away from the sycamore roots.

———

The gray man bent forward and twisted the television knob as he flipped through the stations. He wiggled the rabbit ears, splitting them apart as far as they would separate and then pulled them together before turning off the set. He sat down and leaned his head back and raised his chin up towards the ceiling as he massaged his forehead. Nothing seemed to make it stop hurting. He shifted uncomfortably as though he had grown too big for his chair. Surely something hard hid beneath the cushion, but when he slipped his hand along the sides all he could feel was grit and a few crumbs that now stuck beneath his fingernails. "No change," he thought and wiped his sweaty palm on his pants. With very little effort he shook his shoes free and rested his stocking feet on the coffee table. His foot slid aside the leash that had been strewn across the top.

He stared into the black television screen and sank inertly into the blank picture box. As the minutes ticked by his thoughts meandered, pushing him further away, slowly slipping past his reflection. *Every Friday was payday and the banks, for there were at least three in the plain town, overflowed. By the end of the workday there was always a long snaky line at each teller and the mental counting of money was as reverent as Annunciation Day prayers in church. But the gray man never cashed his government check with the rest, and when it was time he would take the yellow dog on a lead and walk to town. The red leash was wrapped around the post in front of the bank where the gray man kept his important papers. Sometimes the dog would lie in the sun and other times it would sit patiently until the lead was untied and the thumping of its tail would send dust flying every-which-way. It didn't mind the man making him wait because he trusted him and knew he would soon come back to unravel the leash, and then they would trundle back up to the broken house.*

"Damn dog!" He pushed it harder. The leash dangled loosely over the edge and with another intentional shove it dropped to the floor. He scowled with contempt. It was red, not his first choice of colors, but in the store he figured it was the kind of thing he could misplace, and if it was red it just might be easier to locate. The dog didn't take to it at first and pulled in all and any directions. But the gray man was patient and with time tamed the dog into knowing it was only used for walks about the town. All other occasions it was free to roam. He hated to admit it, but he missed the dog and speculated it may have wandered up to the house on the top of the hill. He hoped not. "I'll check it out in the morning," he thought, and with a grimace of disgust groaned again from the pain brought on by his stupidity.

———

But the dog wasn't at the house on the top of the hill. Rather, it had hitchhiked from town to the diner. It was standing by the side of the road, rather scraggy looking at first for its hair was matted from mud on the under-belly, but it seemed as though it was smiling, for its mouth was slightly ajar and showed just a glint of teeth. The red pick-up truck stopped and when Doug Fairbanks, an industrious young man on his way to a plumbing job, opened the passenger door with the full intention of letting the dog jump in, it did just that. And that's how it got to the diner.

It wasn't the first time the dog managed to find its way to the diner having frequently accompanied the gray man on his restless rambles. Today it was alone and as soon as the truck stopped and the driver's door was opened, it lunged forward, leaping across the driver and scrambling out before the man could yell, "Stop!" But the dog was on a mission, and having smelled the familiar odors before, followed its nose round to the back and directly to the garbage.

The pick-up truck's driver had no intention of going after the hitchhiker, but only to trail it with a solicitous eye while it scampered out of view. Born and raised in the plain town, Doug Fairbanks worked as an apprentice all through high school. The fruits of his labor rewarded him now as a master plumber. He was a self-made man, owned his own tools, business cards, and in four years his truck too.

"Thank the Lord you're here!" Pearl latched onto his arm and escorted him into the kitchen. Her hushed voice signaled that such a travesty was not to be detected by the patrons. "The sink in the kitchen has been running slow for a few days and to tell you the truth, honey, it's got to be the grease. I've been warnin' Connie to stop pouring it down the drain; on account of I had the same problem at home. You remember, don't you? Or was it your daddy that came to fix it; I never do remember these things." The waitress smiled and without taking another breath started again. "Anyway, Connie should of takin' the can out back and dumped the whole damn thing into the garbage like we used to, but when it gets cold, well, you know, it's just too nippy to take it out. We sure hope you can fix it, lickety-split before the lunch crowd!" She pointed to the problem.

He bowed forward, leaning into the large porcelain sink and then frowned as if peering under a manhole cover. A layer of brown grease and discards were still floating, hiding murky dishwater that filled the bottom-half with submerged crockery buried beneath like carcasses. "So, what do you think? Kind of a mess, isn't it?" She giggled and as though taking a dare, poked and split the film with her index finger.

"I've seen worse." The plumber, with an air of authority, pulled from his bag a few tools while the waitress hinted a sigh of relief as if she had been absolved of a crime.

"Oh, that's encouraging! So, how long will it take to fix 'cause I want to get it unclogged before Connie gets back." From beneath the cabinet there could be heard the repositioning of a tin bucket and the scratching of a wrench against the old pipe. Flakes of rust splintered off like wood shavings.

"Give me an hour and I'll have you back up and running."

"An hour! That long?"

But before she could complain again, the man slid out from beneath the cabinet holding up an elbow joint stuffed with a clump of matted hair. "The life of the sink depends upon a healthy drainpipe, and it appears that yours has come down with a severe case of arteriosclerosis! I think we can assume that unless some animal was trapped, there's more than grease that's clogged your sink." His eyes met the woman's and by her vacant expression knew something was amiss.

"I've been caught!" she confessed and with a shrug twirled her hair around her finger. "Now be a sweetie and don't tell; I forgot to pay my 'lectric and a girl can hardly go without hot water! I promise I'll never dye my hair in the restaurant sink again. Cross my heart!" She gave him a wink and trusted this signal would humor him as to not divulge her secret, but he had already slid back under the sink. Among the forces in her reach was the ability to make unpleasant things seem all right using her unmitigated self-assurance. Outside several cars and trucks were making their way in and out of the parking lot. She paused for a moment, rearranged her apron, and then striking a flirtatious smile sauntered out of the kitchen.

———

The dog was sitting by the red truck when the plumber returned. Its muzzle was damp and its breath was sour from rummaging through the trash pails. Fairbanks lifted his tool bag into the truck-bed and secured it beneath the canvas. "I have a mind to stick you back here." The dog thumped its tail against the earth and licked the man's hand affectionately. It was hard to turn such gratitude away. He gave the dog a light pat on the head and opened the door. "Well, come on then," he said. With an athletic jump, the hound scampered across the seat and sat down beside him with full intentions of riding back into town.

Seven

THE APARTMENT DWELLER

Pearl rented the apartment above the store owned by Thelma and Gene Fine. Most people refer to it as "the five and ten" and some didn't even know the real name, *Fine's Dime Store*. The living quarters on the upper floor had been vacant for several months, not because it was undesirable but because there were few reliable single renters. So when Mr. Fine came into the diner one day and overheard Pearl was looking for a cheap but clean place to live, he approached her with an offer. No doubt Thelma was delighted knowing the new tenant had a steady job and could pay the rent.

The new occupant's choice in furniture and decorum would have followed her taste for the more exotic; however, she had to settle for what she could afford, simple oak. Yet no matter that she needed to keep to a budget, her one indulgence was subscribing to the *National Geographic Magazine*. Its monthly delivery would fan her curiosity with destinations that were beyond the plain town's imagination. At first she protected the journals as if they were made of glass, aligning them on the shelf according to publication dates. But after the first six arrived the novelty of keeping them pristine diminished. With little regard for the integrity of the magazine, she cut out photographs and framed them, bringing some color to the lifeless walls. It was a smattering of the world past and present. Into her home she invited landscapes, seascapes, even Japanese woodblock prints. There was a sophistication in her choices which she interpreted as setting her apart from the others. She was a modern extension of these foreign places and foreign women. Putting aside some money, she bought from the secondhand shop an oriental robe, and when she slipped it on she was sure that destiny had brought them together.

The new month's edition arrived as usual except with a surprise of an added feature. Wedged between the pages was a world map that when opened made for an impressive wall-hanging above the toaster and percolator. Oceans she had never heard of, countries that were barely pronounceable, and places she recognized from books reminded the dreamer that her life was uninteresting. The following morning Pearl woke up wearing a new attitude. Sipping her first cup of coffee, she studied the map. Then she went to the shelf and rummaged through the magazines. Sea birds from Isla Raza flew out of the pages carrying a most audacious idea.

Pinning the name tag to her uniform was the last ritual performed before setting out for work. However, an alteration to the morning's formalities indulged her spirited side and with a slip of paper and tape she tossed aside the usual. "Why not," she laughed and peeled away Pearl. "If I can change my hair color, why not my name? Today I am no longer Pearl." With carefully scribed letters in block print she pressed hard against the paper and wrote the name, Juanita.

———

"Janita?" cried Connie. "Who the hell is Janita!"

"No, not Janita! It is just a whisper of a 'j', not a hard one like in the word jam or juniper!" the disgusted woman explained. "Juanita, see how pretty that sounds?"

Connie looked at her incredulously. "I don't know what gets into you? What's wrong with Pearl; a nice easy name to say."

"Nothin', it's just that I want to try this out and maybe if I feel like it I might just change my name whenever the desire strikes. Spice things up a bit!"

The man shook his head because he knew it was senseless to try to talk her out of an idea. "Well, just as long as you keep a tag on so we all know who is comin' to work! Say it again."

"Say what again?" knowing full well what he meant.

"Who you are!"

With an over exaggerated pucker of her lips she whispered into his ear, "Today, I'm Juanita." And then she backed away offering a sinister smile. "But I'll always be your Pearl."

"Well, when you say it like that, I guess it ain't so bad."

Eight

A RIDE TO FREEDOM

Positive feelings towards nature were not an emotion that the folks in the town embraced since it was Mother Nature that caused so much of the disorder in their lives. Roads eroded, rains flooded, and the sun crisped the plants in the gardens and farms. Moments of melancholy were commonplace, a condition that was referred to as "having the doldrums". It seemed as though there was always something to fix, something that needed to be tied up, replaced, painted, or replanted. The summers were too hot and the winters were too cold, so any love for nature came from those who had accidentally been in a place where a rainbow happened to arch, a sunset slipped between the horizon, or a full moon trapped between a swarm of stars. Only Matthew Kamer appeared to respect the curiosities of nature, and perhaps that is why his garden always flourished.

The dog was not at the house on the hilltop, Kamer explained apologetically to the gray man the next morning. "I am afraid you've wasted your time coming on up here." The old man smiled as he stood in the doorframe of his lovely white house.

"Don't apologize, it was worth a try." But something resistant in the widower's voice gave him a renewed impression of the man.

Kamer appeared to have noticed the reticent look and added, "I have seen it around here before, but not recently." He hoped to squelch any doubts.

"No, I understand. He's a digger and with your gardens I can understand you not wantin' him here." The gray man looked around and gestured to the property.

"Digger?" the white-haired man suddenly came alive.

"You know, digging up stuff. He's always bringing home something. Why just a few months back he carried home an old shoe. No telling where it was from or how long it was in the ground. Could have belonged to some dead guy for all I know!" he laughed, but the listener did not seem a bit amused by this ghoulish suggestion. They faced each other for another few awkward moments until the gray man stepped back. "Well, if you see him, just take him by the collar and tie him up to your post here. Let me give you my number, you don't mind do you?"

"That's okay, I know who you are. If he comes about I can drive him down to the post office." He smiled. "You're fond of this dog, aren't you?"

The question came as a surprise and even more surprisingly it took him a moment to calculate an answer. "Yea, well," he fumbled with the words. "He is a pain in the ass, but pretty good company, I suppose," and noticing he had evoked a smile from the elder decided to take this as winning a few points. "Well, thanks for your time."

"No bother, no bother at all. Good luck finding your dog." He stood and waited as the visitor stepped down from the porch and then with a perfunctory wave he shut the door.

By chance it happened to be a rather noteworthy day; the air was crisp and the cloudless sky resembled more of a watercolor where both tranquility and peace had been fenced in around the hill. However, even amongst this unexpected bit of perfection, the gray man trundled down the driveway never stopping to admire his surroundings; he never took the time to glance upon the landscape, the trees, the flowers, or the simple headstone of Mrs. Kamer's. All he could think about was why the hell he had decided to park his station wagon at the bottom of the hill.

———

How one's character is judged can often be siphoned into a well of undeserving observations; sometimes self-inflicted and sometimes by unavoidable situations. For almost a month now Jessie had been sleeping in her car, and though it provided the independence she craved, she knew that she would not be able to keep up the charade for too long; the charade that everything was all right. The plain town didn't ask any questions, but the people that lived in it did. The strain of pretending to be someone she wasn't had chipped away her youthful patina, exposing a more polished and seasoned demeanor. But whatever the past may betray, it was becoming perfectly clear that the recent weeks in the company of new people had aroused a dormant feeling of confidence. She looked at things differently now, decisions were made on the spur of the moment, and truth could be breached with a nod of yes or no.

The blue truck sparkled beneath the blanket of parking lot lights. She placed the driver's order of meatloaf and mashed potatoes on the table, asked him if he wanted extra gravy on the side, and then stood restlessly, the empty tray nestled under her arm while contemplating her next move. She pulled the pad from her apron pocket, glancing down just long enough to catch him looking at her legs. "Anything to drink with that?" She could tell he was interested.

"Coffee, just coffee."

"Coffee," she repeated as she wrote the order. "Got cream and sugar here," she added tapping the sugar container with her pencil, and then turned quickly away so as not to appear too interested. She could feel him tracing her steps back to the kitchen.

Pearl, (who on this day was still masquerading as Juanita) was too busy to pay her any mind and Jessie was glad of that. Pearl's ability to uncover another's thought was an art that the young waitress had just recently discovered the woman possessed. The seasoned waitress could extract information with just a glint of a question. And though she was a bit odd, seeing as she enjoyed changing her name which seemed to coincide with the phases of the moon, her talent to size-up a person had been honed and refined for years. So when hungry patrons entered the diner she could figure out what they were going to order or what was on their minds. "See that guy there, the one with the mustache, pork chops." And sure enough in the next fifteen minutes he was eating a plateful; or, "Watch out for the skinny guy there, on the rebound," she would mutter under her breath. Jessie leaned against the counter and wondered if the waitress could expose anything about the driver of the blue truck, but thought better of asking her.

She eyed the rear of the diner feeling more like the color white in a rainbow. Juanita was parading from table to table, her behind swayed as she walked and the customers enjoyed all of her. She was indeed the mistress of the restaurant, and although the more matronly one, she was clearly the most popular. The younger found herself envying the redhead.

"Hey kid! What's wrong with you? I've been ringin' this damn bell, pick up!" Connie pointed to "the blue-plate specials", platters of gravy-smothered meatloaf with a side of string beans and mashed potatoes. Pressed into each lumpy mound was a thumb-size depression plugged with melting butter like a greasy dimple. The opening into the kitchen exposed the irritated cook; his face flushed and his underarms stained with sweat. Steam was rising from a pot of boiling water, bubbling angrily, and the iron griddle sizzled and spattered with the fat of frying meat. It was a voiceless hodgepodge of protests and complaints. "Let's go, Jane, let's go!" The impatience in his voice resonated with each gestured finger pointing at the lineup of platters.

"Shit, when will he get my name right?" Annoyance at his stupidity stirred her emotions. She could feel a bit of sarcasm wanting to escape, but held back any comment that might turn ugly. "Sorry, Connie." She balanced the crockery across one arm and snatched up the coffee in the other. The gravy sloshed about the plate and slid over the rim onto her folded fingers.

"Don't let him get to you," whispered Juanita who intercepted the girl's resentment as she was heading towards the customer. "He's just mad 'cause he had to pay the plumber; hates to part with money, the old skinflint."

The younger woman nodded that she had heard and set the platter down before the man. "Sorry about the wait." Her eyes roamed his finger for a wedding ring. "Single or a liar," she decided. His hands were tanned and rugged but his nails were fairly well-groomed for a truck driver. She wanted to say something witty, something that would flaunt her sophisticated side. "Bon appétit!"

He smiled, thanked her for the meal, and picked up his knife and fork. She turned and walked away shuddering at her remark. "Bon appétit, bon appétit, shit, what the hell was I thinking!" But if the young man heard the phrase or not it didn't matter for he was relishing his meal as if it had been cooked by his own grandmother.

———

The dog loitered by the side of the road as Doug Fairbanks drove away. It sniffed its surroundings and set off in the opposite direction of the red truck. A tarnishing sky lay ahead and as the dog trundled along it stopped every few yards to smell the air. The wind was light and damp and carried with it the loneliness of the night. It walked with his head bowed until it came to a puddle and stopped to lap up the water. And then when it was not thirsty any more the dog looked up and turned towards the lights in the distance and headed slowly up the hill.

Nine

FISH, FISHERMAN, AND THE DOG

There were folks living in the plain town that had never seen the ocean. To some, it was as exotic a notion as a trip to China. "Let's go somewhere absolutely different." Jen's suggestions were fanned out over the coffee table; pamphlets she had been collecting over the years. Their wrinkled edges and dog-eared pages subtly expressed her desire to travel.

JJ picked one up. "Discover the beaches of Pensacola," it announced in bold orange lettering. "Pensacola? Pensacola, Florida?"

Jen knew that voice; it was the same tone that came right before the excuses why a different restaurant should not be tried. But this time her mind was made up, she had never been to the beach and it was time. "Yes, it would be fun. Just think of it; quiet, calm, relaxing, a place where we could actually go and not worry about taking anything with us except a change of underwear."

"Just underwear?" the larger woman tossed the pamphlet aside.

"Oh, you know what I mean. Come on, just think of it, we could lock up the house and just drive south until we hit water." There was an unexpected urgency in her decision that even made her wonder why the sudden interest in the beach.

"You know, I have a confession, I don't know how to swim." JJ's admission, however, did not come as a surprise. She waited

44

and then started again, "No really, I can't swim. In fact, I really hate the water." Again the reaction she was looking for was not returned. "It's the fish; I'm afraid of sharks. Actually, that is not totally true; it's because of my late husband, you know, the fisherman."

Jen looked up at her skeptically. "Fisherman?" She was contemplating the scene, the small house on the river, the dirt road and curious blue-black sky after dusk. The river noises of insects and minnows, water slapping the side of the dock, that forever constant movement. The image stirred her memory as she vaguely remembered as a young girl overhearing that the man had fallen overboard, but no one ever talked about it after they dredged. Her mother suggested that he made up the whole thing and was living the highlife somewhere in Mexico. But this was today and she never made the connection with her vacation suggestion and JJ's past. The whole incident was tragic and now the younger woman was growing angry with herself for forgetting, for being insensitive, even if it was so many years ago.

"Yes, and every night he would come home smelling so damn disgusting. I hate fish. I hate anything that swims; except maybe a seal, small seals that don't bother anyone."

Jen scooped the pamphlets into a single pile. "Maybe this wasn't such a good idea. Besides, you and me in bathing suits; now that would be something!" She laughed and turned to her cousin. But it was too late; a distant expression had taken over the woman's face, a strange look that Jen had never witnessed or perhaps had never noticed.

A flowering out of nervous tension emerged as the distracted woman tried to regain her composure. "I like the color of water, the blues and silvers, you know, even when it is green. Green from the algae; it's just the smell and the blood. I don't suppose you know just how much blood there is when fish are cut up." She shook her head sorrowfully, "Just so damn much of it. Maybe that's why the sea is so big, to soak up all that blood."

Jen got up from her seat and sat in close to JJ. She placed her hand on the back of her bowed head and tapped it gently. "Maybe." she agreed and stroked her hair. "Maybe."

———

Beneath the gray tints of nightfall, the dog followed his nose up the hill. The clouds pushed by an untroubled breeze shifted restlessly and like taking up a strategic position, they settled themselves above the plain town. With not much more warning than a rumble of thunder the rain began to fall, and as if an egg had been cracked into a skillet, the drops splattered upon all that lay below.

The dog was wet when he reached the top of the hill. Its fur was of the kind that seemed to repel water as feathers of a duck are designed to do, however, even its yellow coat could not protect him from this storm. He roamed about with an eye towards shelter until he came upon the door of the work-shed still slightly ajar; and the opportunist as he was, he pushed it open. Although the interior was filled with the usual gardening tools, hoes, shovels, a wooden workbench lined with clay pots and a metal watering can, there was enough space to crouch down. The rain leaked in from an unsealed slat in the roof and like a pleading voice ringing in the ears, it never stopped dripping. He lay with his head resting on his front legs, tired ears drooping, eyebrows furrowed, and partly open eyes staring at nothing in particular. In the hour that passed the spirit of the dog was put to rest for the repetitive drip of the rain was hypnotically monotonous, and the dullness of the pattering finally lulled him to sleep.

For over an hour it rained until the land was soaked and could hold the water no more. So it lay on top of the earth and spread like oil, drifting aimlessly, until it found its way into the shed. The dog awoke from his sleep and finding its legs, stood up. It shook itself wildly and the water sprayed everywhere. Then, it walked out from the shed and into the black night. There were no more stars or moonbeams to guide him. The dog had to sniff along the ground to find its way along the dark. It had a good nose and though he didn't know it, he used it to his advantage.

Not far from the shed lay Mrs. Kamer. Like the only bloom in a garden, so was she the only headstone on the plot of land. The dog took no notice of the rose bushes planted in a row, nor did it take time to walk around the small fenced rails that cordoned off the cemetery. Without regard for its surroundings the yellow dog slipped between the railings and trotted about the hallowed land. He was more tired than hungry, so when he came upon a wooden bench that Dr. Kamer had placed not but a few feet from his wife, so did the dog lay beneath the seat. The soggy earth gave way to the large dog, and he nestled within the pocket of soft grass. It lay with its feet curled under its head and it settled its chin upon its legs. A restless moonbeam slid out from between a crack in the clouds and like melting snow it laid across the marble slab. The dog watched as the light slowly moved and exposed a partial bit of the inscription: *Beloved Wife Matilda Jeanne Kamer*. Then, it slinked away as the clouds closed together leaving the dog in the dark, wet night.

Before the sun came up Matthew Kamer was in the kitchen putting up a kettle of water. He wasn't particularly hungry but knew that he should eat some breakfast before his trip. It could take most of the day and into the evening to get to the city, but food was the last thing on his mind. The evening before he had pulled from the closet shelf his suitcase; a rather shabby valise that when originally purchased showed off its fine leather construction and silk-lined interior. But forty years is a long time to own such a bag and to expect it not to disclose any wear was too much, even for this well-made friend. He had argued with Matilda that their steamer trunk did not need to be replaced. However, she insisted and the purchase of a lighter-weight leather valise with two gold latches and raised feet was procured and the trunk retired to the attic. With his bag packed, though he usually had left this up to Matilda, he felt secure in knowing that the list he made should have prevented him from forgetting anything and that she would be pleased. By far this would be the longest trip away from home in over a year.

He winced as the kettle screeched mercilessly. A furious steam was rising to the ceiling. He shuffled over to the stove and poured the water into a cup of instant coffee. The kettle continued to whine, but with much less passion as he set it back on the stove. "The kitchen needs painting," he mentally commented, as he slurped the black coffee. He chastised himself for not having gone into town for cream though decided he wasn't going to let this distract him from his good mood. He had been invited to present his research on invasive spores. There were to be biologists from as far away as Europe; he smiled with the satisfaction of the University having called him; the satisfaction of one who has accomplished a desired outcome after much effort and determination. "*Dr. Kamer, we are all very excited about your findings...*" He mused as he recalled the conversation. "*We would like you to present your paper; naturally we will reimburse you for any expenses....*" He shook his white head in the same way that he did when he was listening on the phone. He had been given only two weeks to prepare his lecture, a rather short amount of time considering the years of work. He sighed deeply as he untangled his feelings and again set aside any displeasure.

———

He carried his valise and briefcase down the stairs into the kitchen. The leather was split on the luggage handle, but he didn't really care much. His eyes grew hawkish as he looked about the room and tried the faucet handles; they were twisted securely. The curtains were pulled together with just enough of a break in the cloth to allow a bit of sunlight into the room and offer some morning rays to the rhododendron. The start of the day spread before him as he made his way to the back door. He wanted to let Matilda know that he would be away for a while. He stood momentarily in the doorway. Where the rain had slashed the earth there was a tear along the grass-line. He stepped down off the stoop and into the blinding sun. It made a little path that he followed, his head bowed, and he could see his shadow walking ahead of him.

"Shit!" But right after the word flew from his lips, he felt ashamed for having made such an inflammatory remark in front of his wife. He kneeled beside the marble headstone and stared for several moments after which he rose and walked in a contemplative way round behind it. His shadow fell upon the gravestone. Clumps of sod and clay had been unearthed, as though whatever started to dig had stopped abruptly for one reason or another. He bent down and began to refill the holes, tossing the muddy dirt back in place and then patting over with his heel. He counted five in all.

Nothing else seemed to have been disturbed, the bushes may have been trampled a bit, but it was not enough to have caused any real harm. The white-haired man sighed with disgust as he walked back round to the front of the marker. He placed his hand on the marble edge and whispered, "Sorry."

Ten

THE MORNING, THE DOG, AND THE HERO

The greatest attraction during a meal is not always the food placed before one, but rather a distraction that takes one away from eating. And so it was that the cousins were sitting at the kitchen table when they heard a commotion outside. Jen reached over and placed her glass back on the placemat. "Sounds like the garbage." She crumpled her napkin and blotted the beads of water that had bled into the material.

"Probably those damn raccoons; they seem to always know when we're eating breakfast," JJ grumbled as she buttered her toast as though using a palette knife. The bread soaked up the oleo making it ready for the grape jelly. The ruckus of another trash can being toppled over resonated into the house. She tossed the bread back onto the plate and slid her chair away from the table. "Damn it!"

Jen looked over at her cousin to see what expression she was wearing. It was perfectly neutral, in an unnatural sort of way. "Let me go; you might do something that you'll later regret."

"What's that supposed to mean?" But she knew quite well what was intended by the statement; for her temper sometimes forged ahead of her rational.

Jen walked over and patted the top of her head as the larger woman picked up her knife and continued to spread some jelly. The screen door squeaked open. "Well, if it isn't that dog!"

"What dog?"

"The big yellow one!"

"Big what?" JJ hollered back with a mouthful of toast. "You know my hearing isn't what it used to be!" A disgusted trail of annoyance followed her words.

Clomping footsteps entered the house with two pairs of feet shadowing behind into the kitchen, leaving a muddy trail of dog prints on the linoleum. But before Jen could begin to explain there sounded a protest.

"Outside, fine; but what's that mutt doing inside? And look!" the alarmed woman added pointing to its feet. "It's filthy!"

"Of course its filthy, it's been raining. Poor thing, I'm just going to dry him off and give it a little something to eat." Jen's voice was overly sympathetic, but one could not be sure if it was aimed at the dog or the despaired woman. The dog sat down and waited next to the sink as Jen headed into the bathroom. She retuned clenching a bath towel and comb.

"I guess we're done." JJ pushed her half-eaten breakfast to the middle of the table and stacked one plate upon the other. But her irritated announcement was ignored or simply not heard for Jen turned into the living room with the canine guest trotting behind.

The yellow dog lay down on the rug and placed its head on his feet, allowing the towel to be rubbed all over. There was a loud thumping of the tail and a cry of, "He likes it!"

"Who wouldn't!" retorted JJ, now resigned to the fact that the morning belonged to the dog. She took the dishes over to the garbage and started to scrape the egg remains into the bin. "What are you going to feed it? I know it likes my chicken," she griped, scoffing at her own good-nature.

"I wouldn't think it would be very hungry," Jen started to explain in a most apologetic tone, "seeing that it already had breakfast." The younger woman continued, "Apparently we have very appetizing garbage." She thought that this statement would have aroused some sort of irritated response, but it didn't.

"Maybe we ought to give it the dishes to wash," and with a surprising change of heart, JJ brought her plate into the living room and placed it down before the dog. It sniffed and then lifted its head with interest. Maneuvering only the neck and snout, the long tongue made several passes over the plate, licking it clean.

The dog lay back on its side as though sunning itself on a beach. And though its fur was caked with mud and its jowl was damp with small bits of debris loosely arranged over the muzzle, its disposition was that of a very nice dog.

The morning was off to a cozy start, as if it should be the end of a long day rather than the beginning. A hint of light filtered through the clouds and it gave one hope that maybe it would be a sunny day after all. Tranquility fell over the room. Jen petted the content visitor and combed its fur with a wide-tooth comb. She gathered the loose hairs and tiny twigs and clumps of mud into a small pile. The dog lay patiently for what seemed like a long time and then, with no provocation, it got up and trotted over to the door. Sounding one loud bark it demanded exit back out into the plain town.

———

The morning passed into the early afternoon. The gray man strolled with a lazy attitude dodging the small puddles that attracted the sparrows like sandpipers on a shore. He reached into his pocket and picked about the loose change before retrieving a small wad of bills. He stopped and counted twenty-seven dollars: two tens, a five, and two singles. He felt rich knowing that he had scored the money in a friendly game of poker. He always thought the dog was his lucky charm, but apparently this was only a myth... his silent laugh roused his emotions. It had been way too long and the ungrateful mutt was still missing. Perhaps it was for the best. An uninvited sensation of guilt and anger stirred inside of him. The two parts combined made for an unpleasant feeling, one that got him reminiscing, and though this was something he didn't like to do, he found himself thinking about the dog.

He happened to come across it as he was driving to work; a scrawny looking little runt that had run out into the road. It was just plain luck that it hadn't been run over, but being that it was so damn early in the morning was probably the only reason it hadn't been hit. He stopped short just in time to see it scamper back into the nearby brush and watched the movement of the tall grasses until finally the stalks stood still again. The wind carried a faint whimper into the open car window. He contemplated driving away but decided to abandon his usual callous disposition. Through the morning mist a silent kettle of vultures circled overhead. He opened the door, stepped out, and walked towards the mournful cry. As he neared the sound, the detail of the scene suddenly appeared before him; concealed beneath the scrub brush lay a tan dog. The large canine's jaw was slightly open, its tongue hanging limp over the side of the mouth like a piece of flat rubber. One of its front legs was gnarled and badly contorted. Two sallow puppies were fixed flat beside her; small, emaciated, with bellies extended, their cobalt eyes staring blindly upward. A pitiful yellow puppy nudged the mother with its nose, but the prone dog did not move nor stir. The troubled animal traced around the large body and sniffed, prodding its siblings, but still no life could be resurrected.

"Come on here, fellah," he called and tapped his knee. The yellow dog looked up and froze. It retreated behind the corpse of its mother and nestled its nose to the ground trying to squeeze between the earth and the body. The man called again, "Here now, come here," but this sentiment only made the small animal more fearful. With several unsuccessful attempts it scratched the ground with its paws and pushed its snout into the dirt. The gray man watched for a moment and then made a heroic gesture and swooped the orphaned dog up. It yelped in horror as it was lifted away from what it thought was safety. With fitful yips its timidity was transformed into anger as it began to snap and wriggle with all intentions of being set free.

"Now, you don't want to be the next meal for a coyote do you?" He carried the shivering pup back to the truck and slid it across the passenger seat. It cried and yowled as though its heart was broken and as the gray man drove away the sun was being pulled upward, torn free from the horizon. He turned and looked over at the dog; all yellow and soft and so very tiny. "Cute little fellah," he thought and turned back to the road. "Come on over here," he said and tapped the seat. But the small animal refused to give him any acknowledgement of gratitude for saving its life. In its misunderstood unhappiness, it teetered on hind legs with its nose pushed against the window and continued to whimper as it watched its world go by.

———

The plain town was home to many storefront windows, most of which were smudged with fingerprints and childhood memories. The gray man now walked more briskly, drawing slowly upon the thoughts he had just conjured up. A low-hanging sign above the covered walkway read, *Calhoun's*. He stopped, opened the door, and peered into the barbershop. A pair of silver bells attached to a chord of braided rope hung from the inside doorknob jingled, which made his half-entry not as inconspicuous as he had planned. Two men seated in overstuffed chairs sat draped beneath barber capes, while the Calhoun brothers stood alongside of their clients. Each worked independent of the other; however, they carried-on as if performing a duet. The two barbers occupied most of the floor space for they were big and portly and enjoyed their food as much as the conversations they directed. The smell of menthol and cigarette smoke was prominent, and it stung the nose upon entry. At each station was a conical container filled with a blue liquid to sanitize the rattail combs or at least give such an impression. Two wooden chairs placed side-by-side were occupied by waiting customers. The older of the two men was tipping back and forth.

"Come on before you let the flies in," ordered Sid; his voice bullish and domineering. Everyone laughed.

The gray man slipped in and shuffled up next to the barber. But before he could speak Sid started in again, "I'm afraid we're pretty busy. Come back in about a half-hour?" He nodded towards the two men waiting.

"Make that twenty minutes," amended the brother. He was swirling a steamed towel round the patron's jowls, a man of considerable volume who was testing every thread of the white cloth with the enormity of his girth. From between the towel-folds a meaningless tune was expelled, but was quickly muffled by another hot wrapping.

"Actually, I was just wondering if you'd seen a dog around here lately; a big yellow one." The gray man eyed the ashtray on the counter which triggered a sudden yearning for a cigarette even though he had quit five years ago.

Sid turned towards him and dipped the stubby brush into the shaving cup and whisked it around as though he were whipping cream. He stirred vigorously as he spoke. "A stray dog," and as he thought aloud the lather began to work its way up the mug. "Yep, there was a dog. I did see a dog yesterday, or was it the day before?" He set the cup back on the counter and with a pensive display of gestures, stroking his chin with the same enthusiasm one contemplates a mathematical problem, he finally acknowledged. "There was one out back by the garbage, but can't remember if it was yesterday or the day before."

"Day before," added Owen. The other barber stood talking to the man's refection in the mirror. "It was the day before because that's the same day we ordered in salami sandwiches and I remember; we threw away the wax paper. There was so much damn paper, a real waste. Had to be; yes indeed, had to be the day before 'cause if I were a dog I would have wanted that greasy paper! So much damn paper!" Everyone laughed each time he repeated damn. "Nice mutt, though. He slipped in by way of the back door and sat right over there and looked out the window." Owen pointed to the front of the shop and nodded. "At first we started to boot his mangy butt out, but he just sat in the sun and we figured what the hell, he ain't bothering anybody. So we let him stay. That's when Gil Adler came in, you know kind of tipsy; he sat right down on the floor and started to pet him, but after a while the dog just got up and went over to the door. So we let him out. Why it took the two of us just to get Gil up and into a chair!"

Everyone nodded in agreement.

The gray man surveyed the floor where the barber had pointed to. He imagined the content dog sitting in the sun and then he envisioned the drunken man on the ground fawning over it. He liked Gil Adler, but with the same degree of indifference as most others, anticipating little and expecting even less from him. Maybe that wasn't a good thing, but it didn't much matter.

"Don't ask us which way it went, 'cause we didn't ask where it was going!" exclaimed Owen. Everyone in the shop laughed again with added jocularity except the gray man who thanked them all and stepped back outside into the afternoon.

———

The plain town was a scheduled town and as the sun lingered above the clouds a few minutes after noontime, all who resided in its dominion knew it was time for the mid-day meal. Like a lone wolf's bay snaking down the treeless mountain, the twelve o'clock train whistle could be heard rounding the bend. The reminders of time were subtle enough and when the church bells pealed twelve, frightening away the belfry crows like a massive black cloud lifting away, one could hardly do anything else except think about what or where to eat. The gray man hastened his pace stirred by hunger pangs and the ruminations of people sitting at the counter shoulder to shoulder, ordering off mustard-stained menus in plastic covers, slipping straws out of paper sheaths, and pulling rectangular napkins from metal dispensers. He envisioned chairs occupied at cloth-covered tables, and handwritten specials scrawled on a chalkboard in oversize letters. But above all was the wall clock that ticked away the minutes regardless of when you entered. Time was the same for everyone. The gray man had left his thoughts of the dog at the barbershop and as he swung open the door he surveyed the diner like a man coming home from a long trip. He sat down at the first unoccupied table. The menu was always same and though he knew it by heart, he read it over as if it were for the very first time.

The waitress floated over and waited as he contemplated his options. "What's your pleasure?" she asked. Her tone suggested more than lunch. She brushed his shoulder and remained close as she bent down to take his order. A scent of lilac rose from behind her ears as she spent more time than necessary in a bowed position. "Haven't seen you around much, where've ya been hiding?" Her voice emphasized the words as though they held individual meaning rather than being part of a sentence. There was history between these two, a history that had ended amicably. The woman was too much of a flirt for his liking, and though they had good times, she had decided he was too much of a homebody.

"Me? Been around; playin' a little poker now and then," he explained to her amused curiosity. Pointing to the menu he steered the conversation back to his stomach. "I'll have the meatloaf sandwich and water." He noticed the nametag and pointed at the handwritten name. "Juanita? You always did like to take on a new one. Hey, remember when you were Lucille?" He waited for a moment, but she ignored him. "Or was it Lucy; well something starting with an L."

"It was Layla," she said.

"Oh yea, Layla." He nodded his head in agreement as he inwardly resurrected their brief affaire.

She scribbled on the pad and then tapped it against the back of his chair. "Heard you and JJ got into it," she said baiting his attention.

"Give me a coffee too."

"Did you?"

"Did I what?"

"Get into a fight?" her voice was hushed but gilded with a sense of urgency.

"It don't matter, now does it, Pearl? I mean what difference does it make if I did or I didn't?"

"Guess it doesn't," she agreed. "Just makin' conversation." She liked to toy with him; he was a good man but needed to be toyed with. "Be right back with your coffee." She sighed as if she longed to have him back but quickly put away any visions or fantasies before they had a chance to escape.

The noon hour stole away the minutes and though the diner remained busy, it was strangely silent. A kind of silence that has nothing to do with sound but rather an internal silence that can only be broken by the intimacy of two people; here there was not that kind. There was no intimacy to be found. He turned to the window and gazed out into the parking lot and noticed the new waitress standing by a blue truck. He edged forward to get a better look when he was interrupted by a steaming cup of coffee.

"Oh, I see," remarked the intruder and placed the cup and saucer on the table.

"See what?" he replied, embarrassed by the question as though he had been caught peeking into someone's bedroom.

"That!" She smiled and tossed her head in the direction of the girl outside. The sun's refection glinting off the hood created a gauzy halo around the young woman as she leaned against the blue truck. Her black hair was raven-like in the sunlight and when she turned her face towards the driver her expression softened. The man reached over and pulled the passenger door handle from the front seat. It swung open. She stepped up and then slid across the seat beside him. The man offered her his cigarette, and she took the half-lit butt and put it to her lips. A feather of smoke rose as she exhaled.

The gray man pulled the coffee towards him and picked up the cup. He blew across the surface until it was cool enough to take a sip. He turned to look out the window again, but only a river of sunshine settled upon an empty parking space.

"Wonder where that damn dog is," he thought and slurped his coffee.

———

The yellow dog turned away from the row of houses and though it cannot reveal its feelings, it would have appeared happy to a watching bystander as it scampered up the hill. It stopped to sniff the ground along the way and then when it found no reason to investigate any further, it proceeded on. In the distance the clouds etched the sky as though they had been purposely scratched with chalk and with the pull of the wind they were slowly encroaching on the blue sky directly above the wandering dog.

He was a smart dog so when he crossed over to the top of the hill he distanced himself from the white house, save the owner would chase him away; for the dog did not know it was vacant. But after a quick lap about the front yard, it soon forgot its fear of reprisal and headed round to the back where it remembered the location and past contents of two garbage bins. The dog easily toppled them over and the lids rolled off effortlessly. Being that the trash collectors were not scheduled to come by for several days, the forager found scraps enough that could keep him well-satisfied; and so they were soon exposed and scattered about as the dog pulled most of the garbage from the cans.

The quiet of the afternoon was broken by intermittent caws which sounded from above. The dog paid no mind to the noise for it was too busy tearing at the greasy bones and gnawing and shaving off with its sharp teeth any meat still attached. But there was very little flesh to be found and so it crushed the bones and chewed the marrow and vomited up a large wad of what looked like raw skin that might otherwise have caught in its throat. And when it was finished the dog wore the smell of the garbage like a rite of passage; it was content for he wanted no more and left the rest of the gleanings for the marauding birds that were circling low in the sky above the white house.

The scavengers drifted downward and sailed overhead scouting the remains before landing, pecking, retreating, and then returning. The dog sat in the sun away from the birds and watched this continual expedition of landing and flying until the shameless looters found nothing more of interest and did not return. But still the dog patiently waited and waited and then forgot about the birds for there was no reason to remember.

———

The ground was soft from the rains and the earth could be easily dislodged with very little effort. Now left to itself the dog was able to chart a course of holes surrounding the small cemetery; and though it had been shooed away before by the owner for its ill behavior, it continued to roam about the hill like a looter. The communion between the dog and Mrs. Kamer had been established by her death and the canine's innate habit of digging.

It simply liked to dig and it liked to push its nose into the holes it mined, sniffing and snorting until it would come up triumphantly producing an object, while blowing bits of mud out from its nostrils, and sometimes it found nothing at all. Here on the top of the hill the ground was especially fertile and it smelled differently than the land in the rest of the plain town. The dog liked that smell, so it dug. And without regard for the deceased, it hollowed out imperfections in the ground; it rolled about until it wore a coat of dirt, the same dirt the plain town had thrown upon the casket.

Today the dog was victorious for among its excavations it had unearthed what appeared to be a flask of the same design and shape that one may be acquainted with in a laboratory, as well as a garden glove. The dog found very little use for the glassware and left it in the very spot it had dredged, while preference was paid to the glove, and it carried the mud riddled cloth off in its mouth with the satisfaction that the day had been well spent.

Eleven

THE SICKNESS

Dr. Hobart's nurse received the early morning call from the mother, a nervous woman who began to weep as she pleaded for the doctor to hurry. And so he did.

At first Mrs. Rosewater thought they were playing a trick, a game conjured up and conspired together so they could stay home from school, since they never took their lessons with any interest. So as she stood by the banister she berated all three and told them to march right downstairs for there was to be no more fooling. But when none took her chastising seriously, she stomped up the stairs flailing the wooden spoon with threats of a spanking for each. However, when she entered the bedroom, what a sorry sight; each child lay as still and pale as a cadaver. At once she knew this was no child's game.

"Never seen anything quite like this; we'll just have to wait it out." He carried a darkness about him as he stood in the frame of the kitchen door. The atmosphere in the house gave way to a heavy sigh. The mother mashed the cigarette butt into the ashtray and lit another. Her sleepless figure was a gray shadow of a woman. "You know you shouldn't smoke," the doctor remarked.

The mother looked up and expelled a long stream of smoke. She nodded affirmatively and crushed the cigarette out into the ashtray that was already filled with lipstick stained stubs. "It helps steady my nerves." She picked up the half-empty cigarette box and fingered the cellophane wrapping.

"When's Dell getting back?" He walked over to the table and put his hand on her shoulder in a gesture of compassion.

"Not sure, tried to get word to him, but seems like the lines are down." She knew this was only an excuse, but it felt good and applauded herself for coming up with such a convincing lie so fast. Lying was becoming easier to her, and it was a lot more convenient than explaining the truth.

"Well, it's just a matter of waiting this out," the doctor repeated changing the conversation back to the sick children upstairs. "I wouldn't worry, though." Now it was the doctor that was lying. Mrs. Rosewater labored over his words but nodded in agreement. The doctor stood for a moment, his black bag dangled by his side, his trousers rumpled and baggy at the knees. "I'll come on back later, but if you need anything before that time, just call my office." She turned and noticed the cuffs sticking out from his gray suit jacket were frayed and she wondered why he just didn't retire the shirt for another. He looked more like a man who had just got off the bus than a professional.

"I will," she promised.

He patted her on the shoulder again. "No need to get up, I can see myself out," and shuffled out the back door.

She waited until she heard the motor start and pulled a cigarette from out of the pack, struck a match, and put the flame to the end. The lit cigarette dangled between her fingers as she blew the match out and tossed it into the ashtray. She sucked long and hard. "Damn, that's good." With her elbows on the table she cradled her head in her hands, the smoke from the cigarette circled around her as the ash grew like a gray caterpillar. She felt numb, helpless; she hungered for a sign. She wondered if Dr. Hobart knew what he was doing. It seemed to her that he did a lot of talking, but not much doctoring. He hadn't been up there for very long. The mother mashed the cigarette out and walked over to the stove. She picked up the percolator and poured more coffee into her cup and tried to recall when it was that she had made it. She couldn't remember.

She sipped the coffee, cold and black. With a toss of her hand she pulled aside the curtain and looked out. A horde of blackbirds was sitting on the telephone line. She started to count, but when she got to seven one of the birds flew up and they all followed like they were attached by a string, one behind the other, heading upward, too high for her to follow. She let her hand fall and the curtain folded closed. She stood motionless. Something was whirling; a repetitive spinning noise had found its way into the kitchen from upstairs and for a brief instant her heart leaped with hopeful anticipation, but then she recognized it as Murray, the hamster, running on his wheel. He was a small, brown and white creature that provided occasional entertainment to the children. Belonging to the three, they took turns tormenting it. So, it was not uncommon for one of the boys to declare it was missing, only to discover days later that it had been accidentally forgotten in a box, in the toy chest, or rubbish bin. But it must be a very lucky hamster having been born with a good set of vocal chords, for surely had it not been able to pronounce its displeasure by squeaking so loudly, it would have perished long ago.

———

Matthew Kamer glanced at the sheet of paper and smiled. He had picked up at least a half-dozen or more that had been stacked on the table next to the welcome sign. He looked for his name and found it: "Dr. Matthew Kamer, leading authority on exotic spores, viruses, and bacteria." Leading authority, he liked the way that phrase sounded. He placed his finger over the two words and then did something he himself could not believe, he kissed the paper.

Horrified by his own innocent yet rather disturbing act, he tossed the paper aside and got up from the bed. He was sweating. It was not a sweat from being hot, but rather a sweat from being confused or troubled. He splashed cold water over his face and looked into the bathroom mirror at a pale old man. "What you need is a good night's sleep," he told the reflection. "Yes, you, the authority…" he paused. "No, you, the leading authority. Tomorrow you will share your findings, and then the next day, and the next day." He stopped, grinned, and walked back into the room and pushed his papers aside. It was a large bed, bigger than the one at home. He pulled the spread back and lifted one of the two pillows arranged side by side, and laid it on top of the other. He placed his reading glasses on the nightstand and then he lay down. This was only the first of several hotels he would stay in. He tossed his itinerary over in his mind, three conferences in three different cities, and he was the only leading authority on spores, viruses, and bacteria to be speaking.

Matthew Kamer set the alarm. He would nap till six and then get up for dinner. He turned off the lamp and stared up at the ceiling. In the lightless room the pallid wallpaper assumed the color of slate. There was a musty but familiar smell and he wondered how he was going to fall asleep. He sniffed again recognizing a musky odor of mold. "Could be in the carpet or the wallpaper," he guessed. "Probably the carpeting; most likely stachybotrys chartarum," he concluded and sniffed the air again. He leaned half-way out of the bed and peered along the floor. The carpet was hunter green and black, mottled with an irregular design that had been worn down and now devoid of any original pile. "Well, it is only one night. Won't kill me," he sighed. He rolled back up, tossing the cover over him but keeping his feet sticking out. He was wearing two mismatched socks and wondered if he brought the other mismatches with him. *He closed his eyes and watched his wife retreating in and out of the house wearing her kitchen apron and her hair pulled back in a neatly woven bun. They sat down to breakfast and then every so often she would get up and flit about the table refilling his coffee cup or serving more jam. He slipped on his white coat and she followed with a basket full of flasks and corks. The damp mist polished their shoes as they walked and from time to time she would have to clean the mud away.*

"Are you finished with this?" her eyes met his, and she watched him adjust the sliver of glass beneath the eyepiece.

"Just let me try one more thing." He dipped the glass rod into the flask and then over the shallow dish. The pinkish jelly turned gray. "One more…." his voice trailed off and he held his hand out for another. She wiped the glass rod with her apron and waited while he stepped away from the table and located a corked tube. "This ought to do it," he mumbled. She passed him the rod. He repeated the action with another disc.

She stood waiting and after a while she asked, "Do you need anything?"

"No, you go on in. I'm just about finished here for the day."

"Well, okay, I'll just take these in to wash." She gathered up the flasks and one by one lay them in the wicker basket as if she were collecting eggs.

His eyes were now adjusted to the colorless room. He knew he would not be able to rest but feigned sleep. He twisted his head and read the clock's face. "Only two more hours and I can eat."

———

The yellow dog never found a way into the chicken coop. It ran behind the west-side of the white house on the hill; an enclosed structure constructed from hewn lumber and chicken wire. A twelve-inch-deep trench dug below the ground was reinforced with corrugated tin; a preventive measure to keep burrowing predators from unwanted entrance. The yellow dog scouted the perimeter of the oversized structure, stopped, and sniffed at the latched gate. He pawed the ground and then gave out a friendly bark. Nothing called back. The chickens had all died in spite of Dr. Kamer's elaborate efforts. At one time he and Matilda boasted of having as many as twenty-five laying hens, but then, after the rains, one by one they began to get sick.

Weeds grew up and around the hexagonal wire-holes and the roosts were swallowed up by clinging vines, and you could trace the spindly branches from one side to another. It was littered with corn feed and straw and grassy mounds gathering in the corners. The feathers had all blown away. The dog stood and peered through the fence. A grackle landed on the mesh roof, cawed, and the dog lurched upward on its back legs and nipped at the air. It growled and barked and growled again, running up and back along the fence line. But the bird remained well above, taking little notice of the commotion below. Forgetting its surroundings, it raised and unfolded its wings and grandly flew upward until it was just an opaque blur in the sky. The dog stood still, cocked his head into the wind, and listened. The caw of the grackle faded with the bird. Having forgotten the bird, the dog turned its attention away from the coop. It sniffed about the ground and without finding any chickens or garbage started on its way down the hill.

———

Mrs. Rosewater was still in her robe and slippers when the doctor appeared at the door. Her dull appearance immediately perked up when she saw who it was. "My, has the day gone by that fast?" she asked. The doctor answered with a perfunctory smile as he stepped inside. She closed the door behind him and then paraded him through the house. She ran her hand along the bookshelf as she dashed past, leaving behind a finger trail of gray dust. Used drinking glasses and several days' worth of unfolded newspapers littered the furniture tops from the foyer to the kitchen, and she scooped up from the coffee table several empty cereal bowls that had been ignored. "I don't suppose you would like some coffee?" she asked, leading him into the kitchen and depositing the bowls atop of the other dirty dishes piled up in the sink. She fumbled through the drainboard hoping to find a clean cup.

"No, no thanks." He waved her off before she could surrender to the notion that one would have to be washed. "The boys," he remarked hastily.

"Yes, yes!" Her exclamation rang out as though just remembering the purpose of his visit. Like a winter squirrel she scurried out of the kitchen to the stairwell. "I did what you said. I wore the mask each time I gave them the medicine. But it was no easy doing," she added with disgust. She scrambled up the stairs with the doctor one step behind. "They didn't want anything to do with me at first. Especially the little one; nearly scared the poor child out of his wits." She turned with a start. "It was the mask, you know. Thought it was the devil coming to take him away. I think he was out of his little head. But thank the Lord. He heard my voice and came around." The doctor waited on the landing as the anxious mother tiptoed towards the children's room and opened the door ever so quietly. Then she turned and wiggled her finger for the doctor.

"I think it would be best if you waited outside while I examine them." He handed her his black bag to hold while he fit the white mask over his mouth and nose and then tied the strings behind his head.

"You look like a bandit," she snickered and handed him back his bag. She waited in the open doorway like a nervous schoolgirl as he entered. The room was grimly morbid and it reeked of cedar chips. "That's Murray." Mrs. Rosewater pointed to the dresser. Dr. Hobart peered into the cage where a fluff of fur was coiled into a ball, and he nodded affirmatively. The doctor turned and walked between the narrow divide of the beds. Two children lay in one and the eldest was resting in the other.

The doctor leaned over and pulled back the blanket and then the sheet. He placed the stereoscope on the chest of the smallest child. The breathing was shallow and half-lived. The brother beside him labored with each breath making it difficult to hear the child he was examining.

"I don't feel so good," whispered the youngest; his voice barely audible. The doctor rolled the sheet back up and stared down at the two sickly children. The eldest boy coughed and then moaned.

Mrs. Rosewater pushed on the door and poked her head in. "How are they?" Her question tumbled around his brain. She waited a moment and then stepped inside and stood by the foot of the bed like a shadow. "What do you think?" Her voice cracked under the strain of the question.

He turned to the woman. "I am not finished," and while ignoring her, he lifted the child's hand to take his pulse. It was warm in the room, but the mother shivered as she impatiently watched and waited. The doctor had moved to the other side of the bed. She walked over to the cage and poked her finger at the fur ball. It didn't move. She rested her forehead against the cage and stared in. She poked again and the tucked head unraveled and then rolled back into itself. This made her smile.

Twelve

THE OLD CEMETERY

Some would believe that the plain town was slow, idle, and limited by its provincial setting, dispensing a boorish impression to the more sophisticated visitor. Yet, if the unpolished veneer were removed the careful observer might learn that the plain town was more like a series of small gears in a watch, all turning at their precise and constant rates, moving unnervingly slow through time, just as they should.

Beyond the town square is the cemetery; a properly cared for parcel of acreage that is entered by way of a wrought iron gate. Though it once was enclosed by four walls made of slate, these cut sections of stone had long been scavenged, leaving behind indiscriminant piles helter-skelter. A cemetery is like a picture book filled with characters that have silent stories. Take for example the social status of the residents; they can be measured by the size and stature of their tombstones. This hallowed land is also where the past and present collide for after the Great Depression of '29 there was little distinction among the plots. It was a long cumulative misfortune which took its toll on both the people and their community; yet the folks of the plain town made the best of their providence and eventually severed themselves from the past as if by a sword.

In the utmost center of the cemetery are the gravesites of two murdered brothers. Though the uneven slope of the land was difficult to level, the groundskeeper in 1822 did the best he could. No one was convicted of this unspeakable crime since no clues were found except for a grouse feather that was discovered lying beneath one of the gun-shot men. For twelve years the aged mother would visit the gravesites of her only relations, keeping it free from weeds and placing wild daisies and aster over the two sons every Sunday after church. And in the winter when the ground was hard and the wind too harsh for the elder woman, she would pay the neighbor boy to carry out her adoration.

It had not been an out-of-the-ordinary morning when the Dodge brothers set out on the dark country path, an old Indian trail cutting through a natural opening in the woods with a swollen creek. There was a fallen tree serving as a footbridge and if the water was running high you'd be sure to get wet. It was a long walk that covered almost 5 miles before they would arrive at the site of the newly planned roadbed to help fell the trees that smothered the land. No one claimed to have seen the two when they finally reached their destination; until discovered just past sunup by a hunting dog that came upon them, both shot dead.

The murders cast an unsettling stain upon the plain town, especially since there was no reason for the brothers to have been targeted. All indications were that they had no enemies, provoked no malice, and except for occasional fistfights, the events leading to their death were determined to have been incited by bad luck.

However, bad luck was not something the mother could accept and while she silently brooded she also vowed to avenge her sons. The grouse feather was kept in a clear vase on the narrow mantle and leaned upright against the glass. Its gray barbs and black feathers were paradoxically pleasant to the contrasting reality of the dead boys' fates.

Like a ballad of promised revenge, twelve years languished slowly; until one autumn afternoon the elder rose from her rocker and plucked the feather from the vase. She shuffled across the small room and unbarred the shuttered window. The wooden planks pushed open permitting a frosty wind to enter and exit as if taking exaggerated breaths. Then, with a simple light gesture she slid her thin fingers across the vane and released her hold, setting the grouse feather free. The feather lifted and fell, lifted and fell, drifting away far from her reach.

One day, when the rain was coming down in sheets, gently as summer rains tend to do, Don Colley and his hound slowly traipsed down from the hills. The dog was clenching something in its mouth, which at first was unidentifiable. But as it grew closer and the rain washed the sky clean, Mother Dodge made out the silhouette of a bird. She leaned forward with her once strong torso, now relying on support from the windowsill. And though one might believe her eyesight was poor, she removed the old shotgun from the wall, raised the weapon to her shoulder, took steady aim, and fired. The dog turned towards the noise, never releasing the grouse from his mouth, but the tall hunter that stood by its side toppled face forward as his knees buckled beneath him while several feathers flitted about his head. Finally the summer rains stopped and the plain town sighed easily once more.

Thirteen

THE LECTURE, A FIELD, AND A BOWLING ALLEY

"Dr. Kamer, we were wondering if we could have your autograph." The biologist looked up from his pea soup and balanced the spoon to the side. It slid into the bowl submerging the handle beyond the point he wished to keep dry. He frowned with the thought of having to wipe it clean on the only napkin he was given. The two young men stood eagerly across from him with a pen and paper out front. "We were at your lecture and hoped that you wouldn't mind." The speaker owned a pair of curious eyes. His had been the kind of childhood spent mostly alone; putting together model airplanes; assembling and gluing small tedious pieces and then laboring over painting with the correct colors and attaching impossible small emblems on the wings.

Kamer understood these eyes. "Certainly," he said in an almost apologetic tone and pushing aside the bowl he took the paper. The spoon slid farther into the soup. "And who should I make this out to?"

"Nat...no make that Nathaniel, Nathaniel Brookings." Kamer began to write on the paper; it was a copy of his biography and scientific contributions available at the lecture.

The other eager student offered him his sheet. "Jean Francois."

"Jean Francois," repeated Kamer. This fellow's eyes were deep set, much darker than his friends, almost black. His youthful days were occupied outdoors, inspecting beetles and centipedes and all things that crawled. He liked to catch fireflies in the summer, only to set them free before he went to bed and later dreamed of catching more the next day. The biologist wrote the name, but not before asking, "So what did you think?"

"Quite exciting!" exclaimed Nat, the shorter of the two. "Especially the part where you explained how you discovered that the virus continued to thrive even after a considerable amount of time without a host."

Kamer nodded approvingly at the response. He suspected that most young and impressionable students would find this intriguing.

"I do hope you continue to explain your findings," the other added with visible interest.

"Explain?" the biologist questioned.

"What he means is," pointing to Jean, "do you think the virus is so virulent that it could one day spread out of control?" Nat folded his arms across his chest quite pleased with his candid approach.

Kamer smiled politely concluding their conversation and handed the autographed paper back to Jean. "I like to see young minds working. We need more research biologists." The two men who had gathered by the table stood awkwardly for a moment and then thanked the scientist for his trouble before dispersing into the back of the restaurant like a pair of shadows.

The patron slid the soup in front of him. The spoon had now sunk like a capsized ship. He fished it out with his fingers and wiped the handle dry. He sipped the lukewarm soup feeling a bit like a celebrity. His thoughts flitted back to the young man's comments. However, it was one that needed to remain buried for it was not pertinent to his discovery. He was the scientist that uncovered the virus's existence, and though it may have been by chance while trying to find a cure for his poor sickly chickens, the known facts were now credited to him. He finished his soup and looked about for the waiter. He signed wearily and wondered if it had been worth it all, but he couldn't think of that now, it wouldn't bring her back.

———

The driver in the blue truck had become more than a regular patron; and though they did not have a serious relationship the starry-eyed waitress was beginning to mentally domesticate him. A beer after work, a drive out of town, or breakfast somewhere other than the diner, her heart raced when she imagined them together. She found herself drawn to the man, thinking about him even when he wasn't around. Without a hint of arrival, he would trespass into her thoughts and then she would find herself daydreaming out the window and drifting down the road. And though she recognized she was falling for him, she was careful not to let him know; men like him didn't like to hear that sort of thing.

The yellow dog sat at her feet by the open car door. She leaned forward and rubbed its soft muzzle and allowed it to lick her face. "You're a damn nice dog; if I had a place of my own I'd take you home with me." The dog wagged its tail as she talked. "Damn nice dog, yes you are!" she whispered. "But you better get the hell out of here before I go on inside." The dog looked up and with an expression of understanding stood up, and walked towards the alley. "Not that way," she scolded, but it paid no mind and trotted in search of the garbage cans.

The young waitress lost sight of the dog as it rounded the corner. "I could learn a lot from that stray," she thought. She was feeling philosophical and equating herself to the dog put her life in a new perspective. "Yes, that dog and I have a lot in common, we're both independent..." but when she tried to come up with more similarities, her mind went blank. "I am like that dog because....," she thought for a moment. "Shit, I don't know." Disenchanted by the prospect of the day, she leaned over, grabbed her shoes, and slammed the car door shut. She balanced on one foot and then the other as she slipped them on and without having any excuses, hurried across the parking lot. "I'm like the dog because...."

But her thoughts were soon interrupted as soon as she entered the diner by the call of, "Where have you been!" echoing across from the back of the kitchen.

"I am like the dog because we both obey when called." She laughed at herself, knowing this too would soon pass.

———

Gil Adler did not remember leaving the barbershop and he didn't remember how he got home when he woke up the next morning. He lowered himself into the armchair, a tattered but functional piece of furniture that he called, "a most comfortable friend". He remembered walking down the road, stopping for a beer at the package store, and had asked for a bag to put it in. That was as far as his memory would allow. Several crushed cans were strewn across the tray-table and with a light sweep of the hand shoved them aside; a trickle of stale beer seeped out. Another morning.

But this one was different. He sat for a while and pulled at a loose thread on his pajama bottoms. Coffee. There was enough water in the kettle to make coffee, but he decided it was too much trouble. Everything seemed to be too much trouble except today's rumbling was making yet more noise than usual. In his head there was a tongue wagging at him, a lot of talk about what happened ten years ago, about a job at the bowling alley and trophies, why he should have sold the trophies for scrap. He tugged harder at the string, but it was too stubborn to pull off. He had earned the job fair and square and if it wasn't for his mother he would still be there. He ran his fingers along his head. It ached more than usual. "I wonder if I'm coming down with something," he thought and then put his hands over his face. "Dog, why do I smell like dog?"

———

A sprinkling of excitement had dominated the plain town when the bowling alley first opened many years ago. Eager young workers were hired as pinsetters and though the pay was low and the work sometimes dangerous, it became a coveted job. The promise of free games and after-hour penny wagers infused a feeling of clandestine impropriety, something that these adolescents craved. The bowling alley's popularity quickly grew among families looking for inexpensive amusement. Consumed with chores and mundane rituals, this new recreation masked the doldrums of the day. But as greed often overtakes even the most honorable, so did the owner fall under its spell, recognizing an untapped potential. Soda pop made way for whiskey, hours were extended past midnight, and playing for fun was sidelined by more lucrative rewards for winning.

As a result of these changes, upstanding families shied away and a new breed of players assembled after dark like nocturnal animals. They smoked, and drank, and gambled, and when the sun came up and they had all gone home there was no one left except a handful of bleary-eyed boys to clean up. The truant officers were summoned when the boys stopped going to school, but the plain town liked its bowling alley and the truant officers moved on when the boys were replaced with automated equipment and a spruced up interior.

There was a flavor of newness and plastic; arranged on open shelves in size-order were two-toned shoes for rent dyed yellow and green. A framed bulletin board posting top players took position below the scoreboard and a bar that stretched half-the-length of the room could now seat thirsty players who tired of bowling. A jukebox illuminated the corner with flickering tinsel lights and its brassy music populated every inch of the building. The silver player never seemed to stop for a breath as it was constantly being fed dimes. Not readily detected were two doors hidden behind a pair of wooden panels that exited into an alleyway behind the building.

Gil Adler was too young to be present, but remembered overhearing talk about the brawl. It was raining hard that night and the drops pelted the roof with an unprecedented fury. But no one seemed to notice because the jukebox was loud with an accompaniment of inebriated patrons singing along. A girl wearing a tight-fitting cardigan leaned over and rested her hip against the young man who was dispensing coins. "Play a song for me, baby," she cooed. Her auburn hair fell over her eye and she pushed it back with one hand and then placed the other over his shoulder. "For me?" Her lips touched his ear and she whispered something.

He laughed and then drew her closer against his chest. Cigarette smoke enveloped the two like a private booth.

Threading his way towards the jukebox an irritated voice stepped up behind the girl. "Let's go!"

"Beat it!" she snapped. "I'm busy!"

The vamp wrapped her arms around the man's neck. She could feel the intruder's stare. He grabbed her shoulder and with a violent shove pushed her aside. She stumbled and gathered herself up, glanced around, and screamed. The stricken man had fallen against the jukebox and dropped to the floor. Blood streamed from the knife wound and was running freely under the girl's feet. She bent down, touched his side, but only for a moment before she was being pulled by the arm. Her hand was stained with his blood and as she was led away she shouted, "My coat!" But it was left behind along with her bloody print on the wood paneling. Like riverbanks overflowing, a sudden surge of people crowded and pushed, straining their necks to see what had happened. The bowlers playing at the farthest lanes added to the commotion as pandemonium broke out. A slurred remark, a punch thrown, and soon others joined in the fighting. Tables were overturned, chairs smashed, bowling balls hurled, glasses thrown, still the music wailed on. The man on the floor didn't speak or move. Someone kicked him, but he still didn't stir.

"Are you hurt?" asked a woman. She was large and drunk and tipping a mug of beer. She leaned forward and looked curiously at his face. She thought she saw him twitch and called out, "Get this guy a drink!"

When the police arrived they found the manager standing guard over the cash register. He swung a wooden bat from side-to-side like a lazy pendulum. The wounded victim and several other less successful brawlers had been sent to the hospital; there was no one left to question.

"So you're telling me that there isn't one person that heard or saw anything," the detective asked sarcastically.

"Not a damn thing, nothin'. Like I told the cop, the guy was lying on the floor when I got over to him. I thought he was dead. Never seen so much blood!"

"Yea, yea, I heard all that before. It just doesn't seem possible that no one saw or heard anything." There was a general feeling of distrust between the men, however, the officer was hoping for just a bit of cooperation.

"Like I said, the music was loud, really loud," griped the manager and pointed the bat in the direction of the jukebox.

The detective retrieved a ballpoint pen, scribbled some information, and then flipped over the greasy page and shoved the small book and Paper Mate into his top pocket. "Damn cold out," he complained as he pulled a pair of gloves from his coat and heaved a great sigh of displeasure. But unable to find any reason to stay, he lumbered over to the exit.

"Want some coffee?" the manager called. His attitude tempered by a sudden leniency towards the detective's reluctance to venture outside.

"No, thanks." He loitered for a moment in front of the door as though having changed his mind, but instead pulled it open and bowing his head against the wind, charged out.

Shortly after the fight the bowling alley lost its liquor license. For years following, it remained closed and in its place a mystique grew up around the site. It now owned a "bad boy" reputation that everyone wanted to be part of. Those who had never been inside claimed having been present at the stabbing or at least having known someone who had a part in the brawl. Its abandoned lot invited weeds to grow between the cracks and along the building; and the only window was boarded up with plywood. The marquee had been dismantled save a few dangling letters. But after time the bowling alley lost its rebellious charisma like a middle-aged man and finally reopened under the glitz and guise of new management.

Fourteen

THE BLUE TRUCK, THE PREACHER,
AND THE BARBERS

The blue truck pulled over to the side of the road and stopped abruptly. Starless, the expressionless sky made the night seem even more ominous. He liked the girl, but in no way did he feel responsible. He had built no emotional ties and the attraction was purely physical. They had good times and as far as he was concerned nothing more. He turned off the ignition and the headlights. In the daytime the field was a perfect rectangle sliced into evenly spaced rows. In the spring it was checkered with sprigs and leggy sprouts, in the summer it was a blanket of reborn greenery, and in the winter it was glazed in snow and ice. In the night it was no more than a black void. He reached into his pocket for a cigarette and then remembered he had given her his last. He opened the ashtray and picked through the few remaining butts, lit one, and cracked the window. He wanted to kick the habit but never seemed to have the time. He was beginning to feel better as he drew in deeply. His father had died from cancer, but not lung cancer; so he figured he had time before he had to quit. The cab began to fill with smoke. He cranked the window lower and let the stillness enter. He could leave her on the side of the road. He shook her shoulder, but she didn't stir. Her head rested against the glass and she looked awfully peaceful. He leaned over, but it was too dark to see her eyes; he assumed they were closed.

"You dead?" He shook her again a little more roughly. Her hand rose up slowly and then fell down against the back of the seat. "Shit."

He slid back behind the wheel and started up the ignition. The lights shined into the field and he thought he saw something move. He waited a moment as a deer crisscrossed the field and ran out of the headlight's beam. "Lucky bastard." The truck coughed and then sputtered. "Got to check the timing," he thought as he put it into gear. A smell of earthy dampness and oil filtered into the cab as he accelerated back onto the road towards town.

———

The plain town didn't have much to offer except an occasional dribble of hope, but in his adolescent daydreams Gil Adler had concocted a plan for his salvation. Like other impressionable youth, his young mind had been stimulated with embellished stories surrounding the bowling alley. He was attracted to the idea of becoming "a somebody", a person others would look up to and say, "There's Gil Adler, the best bowler around!" As soon as he was old enough he began hitching rides to the bowling alley to watch the regulars. Over time the players felt sorry for the boy and let him play. With grim determination he perfected his hook and after a few years he proved himself good enough to play for whiskey shots. He was earning a reputation as one of the best, but unlike the "glory days" there was little money in the sport and eventually even the hustlers moved on. Everyone it seemed had moved on except him.

Time in the plain town passed slowly for Gil Adler. At first he found that working in the bowling alley pacified his restlessness. Then one day a random inspiration came to him; a scheme to open his own lanes. This should have made him feel quite content since he was not accustomed to having many enlightened ideas; however, his mother made no audible reply when he told her. Rather, she gave him a disappointing look that flickered in her dark eyes. So hoping to get a more professional point-of-view he approached Sam Tillman, the pharmacist. But the man behind the counter reminded him that there wasn't any place for two bowling alleys. "Just one hell of a stupid idea if I ever heard one!" The pharmacist's remarks stunned his ears. "This town doesn't need another damn bowling alley," and he laughed. Not a polite laugh but a loud and coarse laugh. It seemed to Gil Adler that most people liked to laugh when he spoke. That afternoon he went home, drank a bottle of whiskey, and threw his three trophies in the trash.

The defeated man soon discovered he liked the taste of whiskey. If asked why he drank he would say for two reasons, because people liked to laugh at him and he didn't want to dream. Whiskey dampened both. "At least I'm not a hypocrite." He hated hypocrites. He wondered how he had not died from the effects of alcohol since it occupied his life like the Bible does a preacher's, except unlike the Preacher he wasn't a hypocrite.

————

The wall clock had stopped working about a month ago, but he was still in the habit of looking up to check the time. It was the same clock that was in the house when he was a boy and though it never kept good time his mother felt that it would be unlucky to take it down. "Father and I received that clock for a wedding gift," she reminded anyone that complained of its erroneous ways. He hated when she called him "father". But that is what her mother called her husband so it seemed only natural for her to follow. When Gil turned ten he started calling his father by his first name, Shep, instead of father on account that it would have been confusing to have two people in the house calling him "father". No one seemed to care.

"Maybe he don't mind you callin' him Shep because he's not your real father. Maybe this guy is just someone your mom picked up." That was the first time Gil Adler had gotten into a fight. He remembered his mother was called to come pick him up from school. She never asked him why he was fighting, instead she just sent him to see the Preacher.

Lloyd Tritch hadn't been ordained, but he spoke in tongues and knew his Bible better than most invested men of the cloth; so that was good enough for many of the folks in the plain town. He discovered his calling under the tent of an evangelical preacher with dozens of other curiosity seekers. The moaning and singing, the trembling and praising; the faithful and faithless fell upon the floor and shook with fervor, and those who didn't even know they were lost were saved. The next morning the visiting preacher made a pot of black coffee, counted his donations, boxed the snake, and drove away.

Lloyd Tritch walked out of the woods and down the road into the plain town and headed to the clapboard Church. He rounded the side and climbed the stairs up to the belfry and crept into the steeple and peered down onto the sunlit sidewalk. He had always been a practical man, one that was not easily aroused. So he kneeled down on the wooden planks, bowed his head, and prayed. He prayed for two days and two nights and when he finally came down it was the last time he set foot in a real church building.

The Preacher's childhood was not unlike the approach of inclement weather. At the earliest age he learned to be vigilant for his father was volatile like the drifting clouds that absorb all the moisture they can hold until finally releasing a torrent of rain. He was not a man that took to drink or gambling, but rather found little tolerance for small irritations. And like the rumbling in the distant sky and the long breaths exhaled by the wind, the Preacher could detect these foul moods as they slowly filtered through the man's body. During these times he would notice the large forehead wrinkling followed by a throbbing of the temples, all indications that the child should find refuge as quickly as one might secure shelter from an impending storm. Then the hands would tighten and nostrils flare, and as unpredictable as an electric storm, his sudden release of anger would thunder and bellow with rage. One could never tell how long this unbridled clamor would last, but the young child, if unable to secure a safe distance, discovered that by keeping as quiet as possible he could outlast the man's impetuous outbursts.

The father was not a bad man, and even though he showed little affection, the boy accompanied him door-to-door selling Hoovers. Sometimes they would be invited inside where he would listen as his father explained to the lady of the house how "this is a luxury item only found in well-to-do homes." Most of the houses had little finery with just a few scant rugs to cover the planked floors; and the boy found it curious how only a bit of "sugar", as his father called it, could sweeten the sale. Sometimes the child would be asked to wait on the porch while his father finished his business because the sale needed a bit more "honey". By evening when they would approach home the salesman's disposition often changed as quickly as afternoon turns to dusk. With the darkening of the sky he took on evening's velvet personality, sending the boy back by himself and returning to "make sure the sold item was working properly".

Unlike his father, Lloyd was not an experienced man, especially when it came to women, but now that he had heard the calling to do the Lord's work his familiarity with women would have to "be expanded". This, he reminded himself, was his mission, and with the *Gideon Bible* he had "borrowed" from a room at a Charleston motel, he set out into the plain town. He had observed the finer points of selling at an early age and his wares were the gospel. He walked from house to house and wherever temptation was he seemed to appear. And while the clergy and their congregants in conventional churches branded him a charlatan, with very little effort he was gaining a small group of followers. The wheel of his good fortune had awarded him high scores, and as it revolved he recognized that he was a most persuasive orator. On the other hand, it may not have been his impromptu sermons that were so convincing, but rather his unmistakably good looks. Lloyd Tritch was extraordinarily handsome. And so it was that he gained his followers mainly among the lonely housewives who resided in the plain town. Many who had not cared about faith before realized there was more to religion than Sunday mornings. Better yet, they could now be saved even in the afternoons.

A light knock, a curtain pulled aside, a woman sitting by the window gets up and the door opens. He stands on the front stoop and the sunlight showers over him. "Let no man or woman think themselves untarnished;

for it was the almighty Lord that lifted me up, and I too will lift you from your tainted heart and onto the path of the righteous."

The feeling of loneliness dissolves and she smiles. "Coffee, Preacher Tritch? I have a fresh pot on the stove and some cinnamon buns." He nods and enters; his hand outstretched and his Bible leads him from the parlor into the kitchen. It is warm and the stove is warm and the buns are warm. They drink the coffee and she listens, but she is not interested in his sermon or his preaching. She smiles again and a wave of excitement stirs. He opens the book and runs his finger along the dog-eared page and recites. Her head bobs up and down and she watches as his mouth is moving but she can't hear anything, all she can feel is his fiery breath and the room grows hotter. He puts his hand on her shoulder and she shivers; she makes a promise she cannot remember. When he is gone she tidies up the kitchen and washes the floors before the child returns from school.

Gil knew before he ever spoke to him that the Preacher was different, different in a way that made him suspicious. He had never seen him come and go, yet his presence was evident. His mother sang when she cleaned, songs about saving souls and praising the Lord. At night she would close her door and he could hear her babbling incoherently. It was apparent she was happy. One morning he woke up feeling ill and when his mother called him to breakfast and he did not get out of bed, she became unusually angry. He remembered her scolding him, telling him that he was lazy and insolent and if he did not go to school he would grow up like his worthless father. She stood over his bed and he looked up, but could no longer find the sympathy in her eyes or hear the motherly softness in her voice; they were gone. She began to reveal to him a side that he did not know, a part of her that perhaps had been hidden. He was unfamiliar with this person before him, this woman that could not see a sick child but rather an interruption in her day. And so, that was the morning he gave up religion.

———

The streets were muddy and the dog was muddy, and everywhere the rain fell it left mud in its path. The yellow dog trotted along the sidewalks and stopped to drink from the murky puddle of water that had settled in the low spot in front of the barbershop. It pressed its nose against the pane and wagged its tail. Water splattered the clean glass. "Damn dog," said the largest barber. He walked over to the window and tapped. The dog seemed to smile back. "What a stupid animal. You'd think it would have enough sense to go home." The man leaned over and touched the glass. Then he snapped his fingers against the pane and let it pop. He rested his forehead on the window and watched as the dog turned and scampered away. The rain pelted the sidewalk pocking the mud with dimples, and the gutters filled with water ran freely washing away leaves and dirt and mendacity that had accumulated over time. For some the rain was a cleansing, for others it was an annoyance, for the barber it was bad for business.

"What'd ya do that for?"

"I don't want it hanging around."

"He's not bothering anyone. It only wanted to come inside where it's dry. Can't blame it."

"I don't give a shit what it wanted." He sat down in the leather chair and twisted it round towards the mirrored wall. He put his feet on the rest and tilted the chair back. "Not one bit, as long as it keeps eating out of our garbage there's no potential for us to become friends."

The brother listened. He was used to hearing Sid complain but was unsure why this sudden animosity towards the animal. "What's eatin' you?"

There was a pause and then an overly accentuated sigh. "I don't know. Maybe it's the rain. Just haven't felt so good. I think it was the bologna."

The other man glanced down at his watch. "Why don't you get on home? Doesn't look like there will be much business today. Go on, I can manage."

The larger barber rolled out of the chair and took off his freshly starched white shirt and hung it on the coat rack. He looked particularly fat in his undershirt. It was snug especially around his abdomen and hiked up exposing a roll of flesh as he moved. He lifted his arm and pointed to the yellow stain at his armpit. "This is what happens when you work hard," Sid muttered.

Owen handed him his jacket and held out the black umbrella. "Take this; it will probably stop by the time I leave."

He smiled and without hesitation the other agreed with a single nod.

———

All the way home he pictured a warm cup of tea and a piece of pound cake and as the rain hit the umbrella he was pleased that he had not objected to having taken it. As a barber his life was easy in comparison to his father who had spent his life doing manual labor. He had decided at a fairly young age that he would do everything in his power to keep from following in his father and grandfather's footsteps. Mining may have been their destiny, but it wasn't his. He liked to think that it was his conviction that broke the tradition, although more likely it was the accident. The barber picked up his pace and leaned the umbrella forward as the wind tried to snatch it away. He winced as he trudged along wishing he had changed out of his good leather shoes. He looked down and followed the road, keeping his eyes on his feet. They slapped the mud with each step he took and sprayed his cuffs with brown muck. The accident had left many widows and orphans. His family was one of the lucky ones. That's what he had been told; except, he wasn't really sure. His father was in the last group that was brought back up alive. One night Sid found him sitting naked under the sycamore tree smoking his pipe and just staring out into the darkness.

The small house was a welcome sight and as he fumbled with the lock, he jiggled the key until it turned the door over to him. But as soon as he pushed it open he felt something nudge him aside and scamper past. He tossed the open umbrella out-of-the-way and stepped into the warm foyer. A spray of water doused his legs as the yellow dog shook itself with enthusiastic contentment. The wet man stood on the welcome mat and stared incredulously. His first instinct was to grab the nearest large object and promptly clobber the dog, however there was something about the furry trespasser that kept him from doing the animal any immediate harm. "Well, come along then," he said surrendering a pat on the dog's head. "We're both wet and hungry. I have some leftover bologna for you." It seemed to agree for it wagged its tail with much eagerness as it followed the man into the kitchen, splattering the hallway walls with water from its tail.

———

The gray man stood in the doorway for a moment. It wasn't his nature to go to a bar when it was still light out, but he didn't feel much like going home. A flood of dust particles rose upward and flitted about like talcum powder. "Close the door, will ya." He thought he recognized the annoyed voice as a woman's, but he couldn't tell. His eyes hadn't quite adjusted to the dim room.

"Sorry." He let his fingers slide off the handle and it shut fiercely behind him.

He walked to the end of the bar. The plastic padding on the stool was split and had been mended with black electrical tape. He ran his fingers across the top and pushed down on the edge that wanted to peel up before sitting down. The man and woman occupying the seats at the opposite end were caught in a tight embrace. An occasional laugh interrupted their inaudible murmurs.

"They've been at it all afternoon," noted the barkeep. He nodded his head in their direction as if trying to make a distinction even though there were no other patrons. "Early for you, ain't it, Bud?"

He hated when he was called Bud. "I suppose," he said trying to act indifferent. "Give me a beer, make it a draft." The barkeep nodded and shuffled down to the taps and then returned with a frothy mug. The woman giggled, lifted her head, and rattled her empty glass making the ice clink nosily. She lifted it to her lips and tipped the rim back allowing a chip to slide into her mouth. She rolled the icy sliver around with her tongue until it melted. The gray man looked up and their eyes meet with a chance familiarity of having known each other somewhere but without immediate recollection.

She pushed her glass toward the bartender, "Another, hon."

She was no longer paying any mind to the gray man for he now bored her. He swiveled his seat away from her direction and looked around the room trying to act as if he were interested in his surroundings. The atmosphere was stale, and old, and smelled of spilled beer and soiled carpet. He reached his hand into the bowl of peanuts and tossed a few into his mouth. He chewed slowly, the salt tasted good until a piece of cellophane-like-skin from a peanut adhered to the inside of his molar. He tried to loosen it with his tongue, but it won't budge.

"Another?" asked the bartender.

For a moment he wondered when he had finished the first one. The empty mug dripped on the bar and the soggy napkin had soaked up as much water as it possibly could. "Nah, thanks," he said and reached into his pocket, retrieved a few bills, and set them under his mug. The bartender came out from behind the bar with a sack of peanuts. He loosened the twine and started to refill the few empty bowls. The gray man slid off the stool and walked to the door; he pulled it open. A flame of sunlight pierced the threshold and slipped into the bar like an intruder. From the back of the room he heard a friendly call, "Later, Bud."

"Shit, how I hate to be called Bud," he grumbled and pushed the door closed. He raised his arms and stretched with the inertia of a waking cat. He dropped off the step and walked toward his parked station wagon and looked about. A car door slammed shut and a thin mustached man with a determined gait was heading for the entrance. They exchanged gestures of understanding; an unspoken acknowledgement dictated by circumstance. His thoughts drifted to the present and shook his head with disgust. "I wonder where that damn dog is?"

Fifteen

THE BEACH AND POKER

J J stood before the mirror and frowned. She was not a woman that cared what others thought but wearing a bathing suit put things drastically into another perspective. She tugged at the short skirt that was designed to minimize too much exposure, however two inches below the top of her thigh appeared to draw more attention to the fact that she was trying to hide something that could never be hidden. She looked down at her feet and questioned how she had settled for something as uncomfortable as a pair of yellow, plastic sandals. She was now more convinced than ever that the manufacture of beachwear was a man's trick, a way of humiliating the opposite sex. She stepped out of the bathroom and exclaimed, "Well, I'm as ready as I'll ever be!" There was a clearing of the throat and then, "and I am not happy!" The disgruntled bather exited the bathroom with a hotel towel draped across her shoulders.

"Oh, you're being ridiculous," her companion animated. "All you need is a little sun and you'll be feeling just so much better!"

"Who said I wasn't feeling good, all I said was I was not happy." The modest woman's voice resonated with her displeasure.

Suppressing her youthful impulse to laugh, Jen tossed a supportive smile and grabbed her straw bag from off the desk. She filled out her suit in a suggestive way too, but not quite as provocative. "I thought we could go down to breakfast before we head to the beach."

"Breakfast, you expect me to walk into a restaurant like this!" and she pulled off the towel exposing more than her cleavage.

"Well, what did you think we would do? Whip something up in here?"

"I didn't really think of anything except that I certainly won't go out in this get-up!" she frowned. "I think this was all one damn bad idea. I'm just not ready to be seen on the beach!"

The hotel room was growing uncomfortably hot and small. The two women took up a large portion of the room that was occupied with only the essentials to make a visitor feel as though they were indeed on a vacation. Jen put her bag down on the bed and retied the cloth sash around her midriff. "Why don't you put one of these on?" she said. "I have another."

The displeased woman mentally dressed herself in the floral beach shift that was being proposed. "Dear Lord, this is getting better all the time!" she bemoaned. "Let me put on a pair of shorts; that is if I can squeeze my ass into a pair with this ruffle taking up all the room. How did I ever let you convince me that this was a good idea?"

Jen smiled and sat back down on the edge of the bed while there was much humphing and grumbling in the opposite side of the room. She didn't dare turn around to find out what progress was being made, but in a matter of several minutes the atmosphere had tempered. "Now, let's get something to eat." The skeptic had successfully maneuvered herself into the shorts without much difficulty; however, the redistribution of cloth was relegated to the outside of her waistband, giving her pants an unintentional ruffle.

"Let's go!" she announced and with her usual long strides, sallied past her cousin, who decided not to make mention of the unorthodox pair of shorts JJ was wearing.

————

The smell of grease and salt air crisscrossed the hotel dining room. The open windows invited all the restless winds wishing to enter to sail forward, however there were none, and the still morning would have to wait for the afternoon sea breezes. The two women were seated at a table with an ocean view adjacent to a family of three. A young pink-cheeked child was stacking sugar cubes and delighted itself by seeing how tall a tower it could make. Every time the stack would fall the mother would encourage the child to try again. The father, neither pleased nor displeased with the outcome, remained rather uninterested in either of his dining companions, and with his face obscured behind the morning paper sat immobile. Every so often he would reveal himself to take a sip of coffee, after which he retreated once again like a burrowing animal behind the two large folds of paper.

"Do you suppose he's reading or just being impertinent?" quizzed JJ, who had taken an immediate dislike to the neighboring table.

Jen shrugged her shoulders and continued to eat her eggs. "How are yours?" she asked, diverting the attention away from the other diners. She knew that any unlikeable behavior could result in an embarrassing incident, and frankly she was not in the mood for a confrontation with strangers. Although JJ was usually right, today they were not on their "home turf".

"Good," JJ said. "So, do you want to go swimming first or do we have to abide by that old rule that you'll get a cramp if you go swimming after you eat?"

Jen looked out the window and followed the path that led to the sandy hem of the water. "Swim; you can save me if I become incapacitated." Her flippant remark echoed her playful mood.

"I hope you remember that you're on your own out there," JJ remarked pointing to the water. "I can't swim."

"Is that an omen?" Jen suggested. The sprawling surf carried her thoughts to the water's edge where she imagined how much of the cynical woman would actually ever get wet.

"No, just another reason why this vacation could be a poor idea," her cousin sulked.

———

The sun shined upon the shore with voracity. The water pulled back as though directed by invisible reins; churning over and over until it foamed and frothed finally releasing its hold and spreading like melted butter in a pan. As much as JJ would have liked to have found fault, there was nothing unpleasant about the day. The ocean was less intrusive than she recalled from when she was young; perhaps because it was now presented on her terms.

She watched Jen swim out beyond the shore where it was too deep to walk and considered what it must be like to be able to float. The swimmer's flattened body rode up and down with the waves, appearing and disappearing. Sandpipers doddered in and out of the water leaving behind tiny hieroglyphic-like footprints. JJ walked out into the water until it came up to her waist, her arms raised above her head with a fear that she may lose her balance. And as the water rose she too rose up on her toes, which made her marvel that a woman of her stature could even tiptoe.

———

When evening arrived the two women were awakened by a knock. A slip of paper appeared from under the door. "What time is it?"

JJ rolled over in her too small twin bed and looked at the clock. "Six something," she muttered.

"Six in the morning?" Jen's voice was peppered with misunderstanding.

"Six p.m."

"Oh, I guess it was the sun. Our nap went overtime. Who was at the door?"

The disturbed woman tossed the sheet aside and retrieved the paper from off the floor. "Whoever it was shoved this under it." There was a silent moment followed by a more animated announcement. "Well, things are beginning to look up!"

"What is it?"

"A poker game in the bar at nine o'clock."

"Is that all?" Jen pulled the sheet over her head and turned over. In comparison to her cousin, her bed felt cozy. "I think I'll stay in." She closed her eyes with a weariness that is used to conceal a great secret. JJ was a wolf in sheep's clothing. Outside the plain town she was an ordinary woman playing a man's game. It was the excitement of winning that kindled her spirits for seldom did she lose. It requires great skill to be a wolf and not get caught, but that was a tactic JJ had that most other card players lacked.

———

Sagging velvet ropes partitioned off tables for those who wished to play. A small churlish fellow with a fledging complement of hair flattened against his balding forehead was presented with the invitational flyer; it was first come, first served. Admittance was not a guarantee and so any monetary incentive was proven to be a motivator. The man accepted the $10.00 bill and escorted JJ to a table where she was cordially welcomed by two seated men, both in their early fifties, one silver-haired and the other not.

"Shouldn't have had the onions," the silver-headed man said. He patted his hand over his chest and belched. The other said nothing.

"Antacid."

"I beg your pardon," he questioned, suffering considerably.

"Antacid, that's what I take whenever I get something that repeats," JJ clarified. "Then again, a little tonic water just might do-the-trick."

"Tonic water?" he burped. "Thanks for the advice." The belching man snapped his fingers. A swarthy waiter approached. "Tonic water," he ordered.

"And light on the ice," JJ added and winked at her gaseous acquaintance.

"Right away, Monsieur. One tonic water and light on the ice."

The hour was drawing near. The bar was filling up as several dozen players were seated around the room. Table-lanterns gave the room an ambiance of classiness, however, if one were to examine the premises more closely they would find a rather old and shabby establishment that may have flourished in its hay-day, but presently offered little more than a façade of elegance.

"I beg your pardon, Madame, but is this seat taken?" An eccentric looking gentleman with a full beard, well-groomed mustache, and rose boutonnière pulled the chair away from the table.

"Suit yourself," said JJ, "but only serious players are welcome." This caused a bit of a row with the others at the table, all except for Mr. Lux, the inquiring latecomer.

"Certainly, then this would be my place." He smiled frostily exposing a shiny gold tooth. The waiter presented himself and took orders. Whiskey was unanimous except for the belching man; his was gin and tonic.

At the front of the room there was a faint clinking of a spoon against a water glass followed by a clearing of the throat. The noise-maker waited for a few moments as if calling court to order until the room settled down. "Ladies and gentlemen, welcome to *Shay's Bar*. In just a few moments your dealers will be joining you. Please be assured that they are well-trained, experienced, and honest. We will open the betting at $20.00. If there is anyone at this time that does not wish to continue, please excuse yourself now." Silence blanketed the room while anticipation smothered it. "Well, then," exclaimed the boorish man with a loud and exuberant voice, which could have been used for the start of a game of football rather than poker, "on behalf of *Shay's* let me say, drink, drink, and play fair!" A few of the patrons laughed while the majority rolled their eyes at the meager attempt to be humorous.

Dangling from the low ceiling were brass chandeliers offering the patrons a dull yellow light. Words of gibberish drove a few conversations, but mostly there was silence interrupted by nervous tapping from a few of the poker-faced players and someone humming an annoying tune. A composite of anxiety flowed loosely around the room; the shuffling of cards and the sliding back and forth of chips disrupted any pursuit of concentration.

Within the lack-luster evening, standing behind the ropes of on-lookers, stood a slender woman with every appearance of being discreet. Had it not been for her red gloves and the position of where she was standing, JJ would not have noticed her. Nor would she have twisted round behind to note a woman of similar stature wearing the same red gloves. Imbued by her keen animal-like instincts, the red rose in Mr. Lux's lapel seemed more than coincidental. Blood surged to her head as she reexamined the man beside her provoking a suspicious curiosity. She examined the others at the table, the on-lookers, and the mounting chips. Cards were dealt and with hawkish eyes she watched as the bearded man handily won the next two rounds. JJ combed the crowd until she relocated the gloved-woman. The on-looker had not moved her position, only her eyes glinted from the table to the rear of the room and back again.

Perspiration formed on the indecisive woman's upper lip. "Your play." The dealer's voice rang loudly, but more as a taunt than a prompt. JJ lowered her hand and held it close to her chest. Stacks of chips, half-filled whiskey glasses, gnawed cigar butts, and fanned cards; all were waiting, waiting for her.

She lowered her head and dropping the cards raised an eyebrow. "Fold."

The clock face read eleven. The ticking enunciated the lateness of the evening. The room resonated with tension as the gray haze of cigar and cigarette smoke swelled. The crowd behind the ropes appeared only as an outline of dark silhouettes. A hideous laugh was expelled and a gleeful, "Must be my lucky night!" was declared. The bearded man swooped forward and swallowed up the chips, pushing them into a bag, which was then whisked away by a red glove. The man stood up. JJ turned towards him. He was no longer wearing the red rose. Her heart raced as he crushed it in his palm and then tossed it onto the table. She reached forward but it rolled out of range. Her chair slid backward and she lunged, her fingertips barely reaching the crimson petals. The room was stifling. She struggled to resuscitate her clarity through the film of tobacco smoke. A strange absence of voices was present, just a muffling of unintelligible articulations, drunken laughter and feet; the movement of feet. "Cheater, cheater!" she objected. Her eyes wide-open proved futile as she groped between the grayness for the rose. "Cheater, cheater!" She heard her voice fall like dead leaves in the forest. Her throat swelled shut and she could barely get the words out. Her mouth moved, but her voice lost its petition.

Someone leaned over; she pushed back, still they were too strong for her. A pair of fingers folded neatly around her throat and pressed firmly. "Cheater, eh, bitch?" She cried out, yet only a broken clicking sounded from her throat. The hands squeezed harder, drawing closed her windpipe, and as she grappled to free herself she felt not the flesh of a bare hands but rather the soft skin of leather. Imposing deliberate evenness, the fingers pressed against her windpipe with the full intention of committing the act of murder. "Bitch, you deserve this!" And with one forceful thrust she was thrown down onto the floor.

"What was that!" a cry tore across the room.

JJ, sprawled out on the floor, placed her hand over her neck and ran her fingers up and down her throat. She was soaking wet from perspiration. "I died!" she exclaimed.

The light switch clicked on replacing the blackness with familiarity. "Where are you?"

"Down here." She sat up and frowned.

Jen leaned over the side of the bed with a host of questions but by the looks of her cousin decided to refrain from the obvious. "You fell out of your bed?"

The confused woman nodded and pulled herself up. The folded paper that had been slipped under the door was still on the nightstand next to a vase fashioned with a single rose made of red plastic. She picked up the sheet and read it. "Charges for *The Lux Motel* ...." She refolded it and ran her fingers along the edge back-and-forth, sawing the crease with nervous energy.

"What the matter?"

"Nothing, just a bit of indigestion. I guess I shouldn't have had the onions."

"Antacid? I got some in my bag."

"No, I think I'll go down to the bar and get a tonic water." She shook her head and stood up to get dressed.

———

Morning arrived with the rain. The path to the beach was invaded by sandy puddles and only the seagulls seemed to be enjoying the ocean. The grayness of the hour made it difficult to distinguish the time of day; it could have been noon or it could have been early morning. Only the breakfast menu gave away the time since starting at eleven lunch could be ordered; making it sometime before eleven. The two women took their usual table next to the window.

In the center of the room sat the family of three. They were dressed in anticipation of a day by the shore; beach sandals and terry robes. An unoccupied fourth chair was piled high with three over-sized towels with the top one sliding away from the rest due to its position at the pinnacle. And although the mother promised the child that he or she, it was difficult to tell the gender at such a young age, would be able to build a sandcastle, the weather lacked any disposition of cooperating with her. JJ eyed the three as the woman spoke in a feverish staccato while the husband every-now-and-again would approve with a listless nod. Whether either parent noticed it was not certain, for the child had glided away from the conversation taking up its time by mixing a sugar concoction in its water glass.

"It's going to spill."

"What's going to spill?"

"The kid over there," the larger woman announced pointing to the three. "It's going to spill its glass of water." There was tension in her voice that Jen needed to defuse. She smiled and tapped the woman's hand with consolatory pats.

JJ pulled her hand away and looked out the window. It was smudged with fingerprints. She unfolded her napkin and wiped the glass. The wind shook the branches and like a dog it sprayed the rain free from its leaves. Only a pane of glass stood between her and everything else that was wet. Beyond the shore she knew was the skyline but she couldn't see it. "Do you think you could swim out to the horizon?"

"Well, if it was a real line I suppose someone could."

JJ rested her head against the window as the drops flung down upon the pane. She squeezed her eyelids together yet still could not see behind the wall of rain. Its sheet of slate dampened all attempts. "I didn't ask if someone could, I said could you?"

"I don't know; I suppose, except that it's not a real place." A shade of disgust was rising; however, she didn't want to end the vacation with an argument. "I guess I could but I think I would eventually have to turn back." Jen paused. "Otherwise I would inevitably just drown."

"Have you made your decision, ladies?"

Jen returned the remark with a frantic scan of the menu. "JJ, what are you going to have?" Her finger trailed the list of options. The waitress tapped her pencil against the pad.

"The Spanish omelet is pretty good, but if you want a big breakfast I would suggest the hot-cakes." The waitress leaned over and pointed out the suggestion to JJ. "They come with a side of scrambled."

Jen gave the mute woman a light tap under the table with her foot. She forced a smile at the waitress. "I'll take the omelet, and a coffee." The waitress scribbled the order.

An unsettling moment rippled like a wrong chord played on the piano. The waitress shifted from one leg to another. Jen kicked the indecisive woman again but this time perhaps a little too hard for without any warning the head that was resting against the window pane began to slide downward, and with a great thud the unresponsive woman collapsed face down onto the table. The waitress shrieked. The empty plate cracked under the sudden impact and the full glass tipped. Icy water spilled and was vectored around the head and torso of the woman and down to the floor. An alarm of shrill cries for a doctor occupied the room as the dripping of water was muffled by the moans of disbelief.

Sixteen

THE KIDS, THE DOG, AND THE BODY

"They've all gone." Mr. Rosewater leaned against the doorframe. His manner was casual and uncomplaining even though he had a lot to complain about.

Dr. Hobart asked again, "Are you sure?"

"What kind of dumbass question is that, am I sure? Of course I'm sure."

"I only meant that you haven't been here and," he now realized that whatever he said would be wrong. "When do you expect them back?" He raised his medical bag towards the man. "I need to reexamine the children." The urgency in his voice only irritated the father.

"Look, Doc. I know you mean well, but she packed them up in the station wagon and has gone off to her mother's in Tulsa."

"Tulsa!"

"Yea, Tulsa, Tulsa, like in Oklahoma."

"I know where that is," agreed the exasperated doctor. "But that is a ways off, and they are very sick children."

"She just told me that there was nothing that could be done here and that she didn't want to wait around anymore."

"You do realize they will need medical attention; when they get to Tulsa." This additional statement by the physician did not seem to get the reaction from the unkempt man as he supposed. "I would like you to call my office if you need anything, for the children."

"And what might that be, Doc? Seems to me that you had your chance. My wife told me that you had all good intentions, but let me see, what did she say? Oh yeah, you didn't know shit about curing. That's what she said, didn't know shit."

The sun generously beat down upon the suited man and his little black bag. He didn't know why he did not turn away, but he remained steadfast. He couldn't remember a spring morning feeling quite this uncomfortable. It could have been the middle of summer; the way it was so profoundly hot. He fingered his collar and loosened the top button. "Must be nice to just sit around in an undershirt," he thought looking at the crusty man before him.

Mr. Rosewater peered over the top of the physician's head. "Well, look what has come to pay a visit?" The doctor twisted round as the yellow dog trotted towards the front steps except it stopped before coming up. "Mangy mongrel, I hate strays. Someone ought to call the pound and get that thing off the streets. See how it's just standin' there. It's smart enough to know not to come round here. Damn dog."

The tone of the wiry man snapped like wet kindling in a fire. The dog scurried down the street. "I guess I had better be going too," said the doctor, alluding to a departure similar to the four-legged visitor's.

Mr. Rosewater grumbled something that he could not make-out and shut door. The doctor, standing idly as if waiting for a train, sighed impatiently and then walked down the crooked steps. There was something unsettling about this whole episode. He wanted to shrug off this uneasy feeling, but couldn't. All tests administered had come up inconclusive. He could only hope that because of their young ages they would have a better chance. But this could also prove to work against their favor. It was all just a matter-of-time. Anything could happen while driving on a desolate road. No means of getting help; "Foolish woman," he thought. He glanced up at the splintered house and then upward to the top floor. The curtains were drawn. "Rosewater would be calling; one way or the other."

———

Those who lived in the plain town were used to the simpleness of the days. Seasons came and went, children grew up and moved away, and the folks complained like folks in bigger cities. In the late 1800s, right after the great flood, the townsmen voted out the "career" politicians. Tired of unfulfilled promises, they wanted change. It was the rains that provoked such a radical move, a rain particularly hard and particularly devastating. The earth had soaked up all it could leaving the rest to the dam upstream, but it could only hold back so much water. In the past not enough money had been allocated to maintain the levee. The water rose so fast that the folks living on the east side had little warning when the initial breach occurred. Tolly Mattson, the miller's son, was searching for his sister when he turned back to warn others. "Never had I ridden so fast and so furious. The horse practically flew even though the roads were sloppy." Those that heeded the rider's cry fled to higher ground; those who sought refuge on roofs and in the hills were saved. Days after the water receded the plain town counted thirty-three souls and fifteen head-of-livestock had drowned. Another three persons, which included Tolly Mattson's sister, were tallied as missing.

But the water washed away more than life and homes from the plain town; it broke its spirit. Eventually the roads were rebuilt and a retaining wall constructed. Times were hard, but after the flood they were even harder. Those who stayed remained determined to regain their losses. It wasn't until the construction of the railroad station five years later that brought the first newcomers.

———

Jen stood on the platform and watched as the train shrank into nothing more than a blemish on the distant tracks. She wanted to have JJ buried in the plain town's cemetery, but it was only right that she be laid to rest alongside of her parents. Good sense was something that was now just a phrase. Her head and her heart were in conflict. The Preacher had conducted a satisfactory memorial. He was a man of deep religious conviction that offered her the re-ward of knowing that JJ was headed for a better place. During the sermon they had all knelt down and huddled together like sheep. A wail had been taken up by the mourners, a sound that rose even louder than the supplications offered by "the man of the cloth". Was it the rising wind or what the Preacher claimed, JJ entering through the gates of Heaven.

Why she had permitted the Preacher to hold a memorial was a question she struggled with. The dead woman would have scorned the idea. She would have certainly never had been party to it. Perhaps for one tiny moment she thought that if she conceded then JJ would be accepted in the plain town. Or, could it be that the Preacher, even as old as he was, was just so damn handsome. "Impossible!" she exclaimed repelling this intimate notion. "A ri-diculous idea!" Why then couldn't she rid him from her mind? He had been so earnest, so sincere, so sorry for her loss. She cupped her hand above her brow to shade her eyes from the sun. Now there was nothing in her view except a long trail of uncertainty.

The next train would be arriving shortly. Several people sat on the benches under the eaves of the depot with their valises by their feet. A small child wiggled impatiently with its feet dangling, rocking its legs back and forth and hitting the suitcase on the upswing. Under one of the benches the melancholy woman noticed a pair of yellow paws protruding out. Her mood that had been weighted down with sadness and regrets became lighter at the sight of the yellow dog. She reached into her pocket and pulled out a chocolate, unwrapped the paper, and placed it in her palm. She knelt down before the dog. The child leaned forward and craned its neck but was thwarted by its mother who pushed the small curiosity seeker back. "What's she doin'?"

The mother turned to look and then replied. "She's givin' the dog something, but it's none of our concern."

"What dog?"

"Just a dirty dog sleeping under the bench. It's none of our concern."

Jen leaned forward as the yellow dog sniffed her palm, and then with a wide slurp it licked the chocolate up into its mouth. It chewed contently and then lay its head back down. "Don't you remember me?" she asked. The dog wagged its tail but when no more food was offered, it stopped. Jen twisted her head towards the child that had turned its attention to playing with the laces on its boots, tying and untying the strings. The mother stared straight ahead. Jen stood up and wiped her glassy eyes. The road that stretched ahead grew sad, and she was weary. She clasped her hands together in front of her and walked slowly, noting the dull, cheerless colors of the day.

The yellow dog slept through the arrival and departure of the next train and when the sun replaced the shade, it woke back up and moved along.

––––––

The dog liked the sunny day and scampered up the hill towards the white house. The grass was dry and tall and the insects maneuvered about the blades without any interference. The owner was still away permitting the lawn to grow with impunity. The yellow dog was tired and sat in the sun by the side of the road. It yawned contently and without care laid its head on its front paws; a habit it had acquired from sleeping outside on the wet ground. A field of clouds drifted lazily overhead and cast a comfortable shadow. But the animal had become accustomed to sleeping not too soundly, and like a duck in hunting season the yellow dog had learned to be vigilant. In the light of day the four-legged tramp rested in short spurts, favoring overgrown ravines and abandoned sewer pipes. To the dog the road up to the house was too open, and even though it was seldom traveled, this was knowledge that the canine did not possess. A crow cawed overhead, a signal read as reason to move along.

With Kamer's absence a new growth of weeds invaded the tombstone as its clinging vines attached themselves to the very marble that bore his wife's name. The dog nestled its nose into the earth and using both front paws proceeded to dig in the very same spot it had burrowed in before. And although its first encounters had been met by the weary husband's redistribution of the dirt, which had been so handily unearthed, it was met again with the same ease. Just several yards from where the poor lady was laid to rest it tossed the dirt aside until it gathered up in its mouth another cylindrical vessel and carried it into the shade cast by the gravestone. The dog lay the glass down and began to lick. Then when it was finished it returned to the hole where it had unearthed a similar flask and did the same. This went on for at least a quarter of an hour and when the fourth and last vessel was tongue-cleaned the intruder nosed about the ground for water.

———

The Preacher had left a Bible on the swing and a handwritten note folded between the pages. "Let the Lord guide you." Jen refolded the paper and slipped it back between the leaves of the book. His handwriting was large and bold, written by a person of confidence. She wondered if he would come back, and then wondered why she cared and sat back in the swing and let it drift. It was the same time of day she always sat outside and she half thought she would see JJ walking down the street. The lease on the house still had three months and then after that she didn't really know what she wanted to do. She could go back and live with her mother and sisters. The notion of them all under the same roof after so much time was more than distasteful. It was repugnant.

The lazy hour of the day passed wearily. A thin veil of afternoon hung low in the hour. She pulled a cigarette from a new pack, lit it, and inhaled deeply. She closed her eyes and with a gentle push let the swing sweep her along. The smoke filled her nostrils and she let out a long exhausting breath. "You know smoking is bad for your health." She opened her eyes with the glare of the sun striking her face. It wasn't until the man moved and blocked the light that she was able to see his face.

"Doctor Hobart, what are you doing here?" Jen set her feet down to halt the swing and sat up to crush the cigarette out in the ashtray as if she had been caught smoking in the high school bathroom.

"How are you doing?" he asked and without waiting for an invitation sat down in the adjacent rocking chair. His manner was large and awkward for white wicker.

Jen shrugged. "Ya know, good days and bad days."

The doctor nodded with a perfunctory agreement. "And how do you feel? I mean physically?"

"How do I feel physically?" she repeated the question. "Okay."

The pause was longer than expected. "There's been something going around and just wanted to see how you were doing." She said nothing. "And since I was passing by, thought I'd look in on you."

"What kind of something? You mean like the flu." She was bored and decided that he would at least be some kind of company.

"Something like that." He smiled and picked up the Bible. He leafed through the first few pages as if it were a novel in the bookstore.

"Oh, that's not mine. The Preacher brought it over."

"I see," said the doctor and set it back down.

She knew that the polite thing to do was to offer him a cold drink, but since she was about to pour herself a whiskey, decided not to prolong his visit with informalities and kindly gestures. But to her surprise, he slid his black bag away from the runners, sat back, and started to rock. "I haven't been in one of these since," he stopped to think and then started again, "since I used to stay at my grandmother's." The thought must have been considerably unpleasant for an oddly sour look came over his face.

"Your grandparents?"

"No, just my grandmother. She was a very austere woman; didn't really like children, but I suppose since I was her youngest grandchild, she found me tolerable." He stopped rocking and leaned forward. "A real battle-ax."

Jen laughed, "A battle-ax? Your grandmother?"

"Oh, yes, old doesn't mean nice," he attested and then in mid-thought continued, "well, if you are sure I can't be of help then I suppose I can get along." He picked up his bag and stood up. "Don't hesitate to call me if you need anything. And please, don't get up."

Jen nodded agreeably; though she had little intentions of moving. "Thanks, Dr. Hobart."

He handed her a cordial wave goodbye and stepped briskly down the porch steps. The black bag swayed in accordance with his long stride. Jen watched him go down the street until he was at a safe distance away and lit another cigarette. She replayed the conversation around in her head but now there was a spasm of regret, a missed opportunity; she should have told him she was actually feeling kind of sick.

Seventeen

THE MESSAGES, THE BARBER, AND OTHERS

L ife's fragile bridge leads in only one direction, and with every step taken a little of its path wears away until one day it disappears. The man in the blue pick-up was long gone when Jessie was discovered. The yellow dog was the first to find her lying on the side of the road. Doug Fairbanks was the next, and he called the sheriff from the payphone at the gas station. He sat in his truck and waited. It took them ten minutes to arrive. Then the coroner was called to take her to the morgue.

———

"I was passin' by and noticed a dog on the side of the road."

"A dog?"

"Yeah, a dog sniffing the ground. Well, I thought it was the ground, but when I slowed down I could tell it was interested in more than just the ground." He lit another cigarette and fumbled for a match.

"And that's when you saw her?"

"Not exactly, I stopped and then pulled over." The unlit cigarette hung limply on the edge of his lip.

"Here." The waitress struck the match.

"Thanks." He pulled her hand toward the cigarette and puffed feverously for several seconds. Then he let out a loud sigh filled with cigarette smoke. "No," he continued, "I wasn't sure what it had. You know how dogs are always diggin' up shit."

"How did she look? I mean, was she…"

"Oh nothing like that, she was still, like asleep. Actually, I thought she was asleep, but…" He drew in and then exhaled a billow of smoke.

"Thank heavens. I just can't stop thinking about her, so young and with her whole life ahead of her. I feel like she could have been my little sister."

"You liked her didn't you?"

"Yea, she was getting to be a pretty good little waitress. Even Connie will miss her." There was a note of remorse in her voice. "Ya know, she was a runaway."

"Don't say."

"Nobody knew it. She shows up here one day asking for a job. No one asks questions when you hire a waitress." Her voice hinted guilt.

"Guess not."

"Anyway, seems that her folks have been searching for her for some time. What a way to find out about your kid," Pearl said fumbling with her words. "I mean this way and all."

"Yeah," he agreed and dropped his eyes.

"You don't look so good, want something to eat? Maybe a grilled cheese?"

"No, I'm not so hungry. But now that you mention it; I do feel kind of lousy. Coffee would be good."

"Be right back, don't move," she said and glided away.

Fairbanks leaned his head back and inhaled deeply and then slowly let the smoke out. He closed his eyes. "Damn dog, it just kept sniffin'."

———

When Dr. Hobart returned to his office he poured a cup of coffee even before he checked his messages. Like every afternoon they were neatly filed in time-rank order. The newest was from Tulsa General. The eldest Rosewater child had died and the other two were in stable but guarded condition. Whatever the hell that was supposed to mean, guarded condition. Jessie Paterson's autopsy was denied by her parents; religious reasons cited. The father was on route to make arrangements for her body to be returned home.

The dominant thought that rumbled through his brain seemed inordinately callous; should he have more coffee this late in the day? He stared into his cup as if reading tea leaves when frantic shock entered the room with the nurse. "Did you see the note!" she exclaimed. "Pitiful, pitiful, that's the only way to explain it!" But the stillness that fell over the doctor's face did not reveal the enormity of this tragedy or its resolute acknowledgement. Finding her breath, she stammered on. "I knew the children were sick, and oh, how often did you make house calls? But then, when Mrs. Rosewater took them away without consenting you!" The nurse shook her head back and forth gesticulating the injustice of the situation. For several moments the doctor heard nothing, it was as if he were looking into the sun and could not see, blinded by the same light that was able to illuminate the world. So it was with her words, falling on deaf ears.

"That's two we'll never know about," he muttered.

"What's that ya said?" asked the nurse. She squinted as if it were going to help her hear his low voice.

The doctor diverted his eyes in the direction of the voice.

"I know; you're a million miles away. Just didn't hear what ya said the first time." The nurse hovered over his desk with the pot of coffee like a pesky fly.

"No, no more." He waved his hand over the cup. "Just said that those two women aren't being buried here."

"It's a shame, a real shame." However, she was finding it difficult to tear any compassion away from the news of the dead child. She nodded her head, resting the pot on the desk, and waited for a long moment. "Well then, if you don't need anything else," she hesitated as her eyes darted from his face to the full pot. She could tell he was uneasy with the way she had abandoned the load she was carrying by how he shifted the stack of papers away from the drippy spout.

"Go on ahead," he said. "I'm just going to finish up."

"Okay then, Dr. Hobart. Just don't go worrying." She smiled sympathetically. The coffee sloshed as she walked and she placed her hand over the opening with all intentions of catching any drips that wished to escape. "You want me to close the door?" she asked leaning against the portal.

"No, keep it open, I'll be leaving in a few minutes, nothing more that I can do today," he sighed alluding to the unfortunate circumstances.

"See you in the morning," announced the nurse, returning the coffeepot to the sink. A hastening of feet, the desk chair sliding, and keys fumbling; he listened while she gathered her belongings. Moments later he heard the front door open, then shut, and the lock catch. The doctor found himself mechanically thinking about the deceased. He shuffled the messages like playing cards and settled them back on the desk. The plain town had its share of hardships, but three untimely deaths were either oddly coincidental or just very bad luck.

There was a chronic hum in the gray room. Actually, there never was any complete silence; rather there always resonated some sort of out-of-range sound; an undetectable whirr, a low buzz, a mechanical drone. Today the drone was seemingly more prominent. He slipped the messages into the top drawer and slid it closed. He pulled his chair back and looked under the desk. The noise was annoying him more than usual. Even though he knew it couldn't be coming from below, he crept under the desk and put his ear to the floor. A sudden feeling of nostalgia and panic overcame him.

"Shhhhh, she will never find us here if you keep yer mouth shut!"

"But what if she does, we'll get the strap for sure!"

The two boys fit easily under the desk in the old woman's study. They held their breath as she rounded the room. His knee hurt and it took all the might he had not to complain, but the thorns could be dealt with later. They had evaded the grandmother's watchful eye, although accidentally traipsed across her forbidden paradise. The flowerbeds had recently been manicured, but the ball had little feeling for its beauty. The birdcage hanging freely from the standing post overlooking the garden now swung lightly, its wire door open, vacant of its little occupants.

Dr. Hobart stood up and pushed the chair back into position. It was quite apparent that the noise was not coming from under his desk. He wiped his perspired face with his handkerchief. After all, it was he who set the old woman's canaries free. It took a bit of cunning to outwit the grand lady, yet decades after her death she was still able to disrupt his day. Maybe he took after her more than he wished to remember.

———

After the dog ate the bologna it threw up. Fortunately, it was on the linoleum floor. The barber cursed, but just before he let it out of his house, he reminded it never to come around again. It wagged its tail as though having just been commended and took little offense when tossed back out into the rain.

The vomit was enough to make the disgusted man want to throw up too, and he wondered what could have possessed him to have let the animal in the house. His head throbbed and it demanded all the energy he could muster to lumber up the stairs. He was wet, cold, and more than tired. He took his temperature. It read 103 degrees. He tossed his clothes aside and put on a clean pair of pajamas, swallowed two aspirins, and slipped beneath the covers.

Two hours later, he was dead.

———

The dog scampered back up to the road, slipping only once as it quickened its pace. The rain was coming down rather hard and even the birds had noticeably taken refuge in the branches and under the low brush. The dog bowed its head and as the rain threw itself mercilessly upon the beast, it decidedly looked for refuge. A drainage hole in the ditch appeared to be a good shelter, but the water was rising too fast and too hard. The wind had risen, rustling through the wilting leaves. The dog was splattered in mud. It followed a trail between the thickets of scrub oak and found a fallen log. The rotted stump was hollowed out and the shivering animal crawled inside and watched and waited. For several hours the rain continued but at a slower rate and the dog dropped asleep.

When it awoke the sun was shining. It crept out like a bear in hibernation returning from winter. It was hungry. It shook itself and the water flew and it shook itself several more times and it moved in search of food.

———

Matthew Kamer had finally earned the notoriety he deserved, however, he was beginning to wonder if what he did not say was more important than what he had said. The drive back to the plain town would take at the least four hours; enough time to consider stopping for a bite to eat. But the notion of another grilled cheese sandwich or hamburger in a roadside diner gave him the fortitude to keep driving more than the nourishment of food. The road was barren of other vehicles, and save an occasional truck he had the road to himself. This was the time of day he enjoyed the most, the earliest part of the morning when he could do his thinking best; no interruptions, just he and his thoughts.

The lectures were a success; his work was published and the euphoric feeling of completion was beginning to take hold. He rotated the radio dial but no matter which station he chose he could not distract his mind enough to relax. He turned it off and stared straight ahead. Both sides of the road were speckled by an occasional dried scrub and lined with brown fields of newly planted seedlings that canvassed the landscape. This was farm country, laced with hope. "Kids eat free" and "U-Pick 'Em" billboards dotted the scenery. But it was the billboard that read "Prepare for Eternity" that caught his attention and when he drove by he wondered how.

———

Dr. Hobart prided himself as being an intellect, a man who read the latest medical journals, treated his patients with the most recent advancements in medicine, and above all was compassionate. So when he noticed the dog scampering along the road he slowed down, stopped, opened the window, and whistled. Then he reached behind and opened the door, allowing the dog to jump into the backseat.

"I'm afraid I haven't thought this out very well. I don't suppose you have a particular destination?" the doctor asked.

The dog merely replied with a wag of its tail which the doctor did not notice because he was too busy driving home.

Unlike the barber, the doctor did not invite the dog inside but merely allowed it to wait under the overhang of his porch until he returned with a plate of leftover stew and a can of beer. "This is for you," and he dropped the plate before the dog. "This is for me." He sat down and watched as the dog gobbled the food. He took a sip of the beer and placed it on the table. The plate was licked clean. He leaned over and pet the dog on its head. It lowered its nose and licked the plate again. "Sorry, but you got the last of the leftovers." The dog turned its head towards the doctor, licked the man's hand, got up, and scampered down the steps. "Where ya headed?" Doctor Hobart shouted and watched as it trotted away.

There was a long sigh followed by several burps. He shook the can a few times and tilted his head back until he was satisfied that all the contents had been emptied. He sat comfortably, quite at ease, enjoying a few moments of silence. But like the sub-letting of a room, the tranquility of carefree thoughts was quickly intruded upon. He wondered if he would ever share his life. There was a time many years ago when he was engaged, but that ended in disaster. How he could ever have ended up with a married woman sent a spasm to his stomach. His stupidity or naiveté, whichever he chose to blame depending on the day, made him rather skittish when it came to relationships. She was a few years his elder, a good looking woman with a college degree no less. They had dated for over a year, quite happily. But when the private detective came to his home looking for a Miss Eileen Davidson, alias, Milly Townsend, alias Mrs. Henry Billings of Portland, Maine, he was dumbfounded. An adulteress twice, he just didn't know how he could have been so trusting. What he missed the most about her were the apple pies. She was an excellent baker; an art which he later found out she had mastered while doing a stint in the penitentiary for petty larceny; when she was Milly. He was dating Eileen, who honed those skills throughout their relationship.

Today had been ordinary yet the outcome proved mentally exhausting. There was nothing settled in his mind regardless of where the bodies were going. The premature deaths could not be independent occurrences; the mere fact that they died within such a short period of time, as well as all being residents of the same town, had to be more than coincidence. And the fact that each victim died in different locations was simply due to timing... time needed for whatever the pathogen was to overtake each life.

Dr. Hobart tossed the empty can into the garbage. There was more to his musings than morbid curiosity. He picked up the pad and began to formulate a few notes. The Rosewater boy was the youngest and as far as he could remember had nothing wrong with him except hay fever during pollen season. JJ was a social drinker and smoker, over-weight, but with no other known ailments except she had come in a few times with a cold or sore throat, while Sid Calhoun complained of indigestion and heartburn. Jessie Patterson was the outlier since she was not his patient. Age, gender, location, habits; Hobart rummaged through his mind and came up with the same result. It was very likely that the four deaths had no bearing on each other. As far as he could surmise there was no correlation except bad luck.

When the wind blew from the east you could hear the cars driving along the highway, you could hear the trains crossing the tracks, but no matter the direction of the wind you could always hear the doves. He shifted restlessly in the straight-backed chair and pulled his legs out front from under the table. He decided that a dog would be nice company. He decided he would like one that would sit by his feet and follow him around, sleep on the floor by the foot of the bed, and be there when he got home. "Wonder where that dog went off to," he murmured. "Nice yellow thing. Funny color for a dog, though." His dog would be brown, easier to keep clean. "Yes, that would be nice."

Eighteen

THE DRUNK, THE PLUMBER, AND THE GRAY MAN

It was just a few minutes past eight when Gil Adler woke up in the same clothes he had on from the day before. "Shit," was the first thing he said followed by, "I need to brush my teeth." The plain town had never been kind to him and last night was no reason for it to change its habits. If he had a good time he wouldn't know, for at night he generally lived in a world devoid of clarity. His shoes were the only part of his garments that had been taken off. He stared up at the ceiling noticing for the first time a rather elaborate crack that was forming around the light fixture.

"Shit." He sat up and let his head hang down, this time contemplating the floor. He reached under the bed and retrieved his shoes. "Mud?" He turned the left one over; dirt was caked between the sole and heel. "Where the hell was I?" He dropped the shoe and lifted the other. This one had a brown shell coating, as if he had stepped directly into a mud puddle with the right foot. He lifted his leg; mud had splattered his pants. "Maybe I was walking in the rain?" The question stirred, but nothing dissolved.

All memory of the evening was fuzzy. He stood up and headed into the kitchen where a trail of muddy shoeprints mirrored his steps only pointing in the opposite direction. He removed a glass from the sink, filled it with tap water and dropped in two seltzer tablets. He waited while they fizzed and foamed, finally dissolving into a bitter-tasting solution. Then, with bit of self-cajoling he guzzled it, and belched. He ran his fingers through his hair. It was times like this that he vowed to stop drinking outside the house. He was no hypocrite and to promise never to drink again would be in violation of his principles. He was many things but unprincipled he was not.

A used plate and fork from the day before were still on the kitchen table, and he pushed them aside making enough room to cradle his head in his hands. It hurt, a kind of good hurt he thought. The kind of hurt that made him realize that he must have enjoyed himself.

"Where did I go after the bar?"

There was a lot of music and he remembered hearing the same song several times in a row. A woman told him to go to hell when he told her to play something else. He staggered and fell against the jukebox. She pushed him away. It wasn't his fault her dime dropped. He stooped down to help her find it. "Get up you lush, get up!"

He held his head and all he could hear was "get up, get up." But now it was his voice screaming "get up!" He reached over to the plate and picked up the toast. It was hard. He bit into the crust and broke off a piece. The leftover bread was the first food he had eaten in almost 12 hours. He dunked it into the old coffee. It broke the film of cream.

"Get up, get up." But she didn't move. He shook her arm. "Can ya hear me?" But the raucous pelting of rain filled his ears so he could not even hear his own voice. He waited under the porch overhang until it stopped. "Thanks, I'll be leavin' now." There was no reply. He stumbled down from the steps; the streetlight ricocheted off the house. Beneath the

crawlspace there was a dog. He leaned over and peeked. It didn't move. He stood up and staggered home.

A dream? A dog, a woman, the rain, none of it made much sense. The only thing that seemed remotely familiar was the dog. He knew he had seen it somewhere before. But the woman; it had to be a dream. She didn't respond at all to his cries and for her not to have felt him shake her was because it was all a figment of his imagination.

The house, it belonged to the two cousins; yet, he was sure there was only one woman last night. She was the younger of the two. But why was she on the floor?

As he staggered home something was following him. He stumbled into a puddle. The dog trotted past and he cursed it. He didn't know why, but he cursed everything when he was drunk. He tried to catch up but it was too fast and soon disappeared away from the streetlight.

He pulled open the refrigerator door and reached in. A quart of milk was on the shelf but felt empty. He shook it to be sure, returned the carton to the top shelf, and closed the door. The sun was creeping under the window shade. He gave it a tug and it snapped up when he let go. A blaze of uninvited sunlight threw itself over him. Mornings were a sad reminder of the night. He shuffled into the bedroom and lay down again. He had decided that things he remembered were the only things that were truly relevant. Last night's escapade was merely a dream. The only part that may have been real was the dog; the yellow dog.

———

It appears that he was driving through the intersection of Dunbar and Jasper when he lost control and careened into the maple tree; a fine sturdy tree that served as a landmark for anyone giving directions. "If you get to the maple tree on the corner of Dunbar, why Main Street is only a mile to your left."

The plain town had its share of accidents, but the early morning collision of Doug Fairbanks's truck was most tragic. The coroner was out of town for the day, and so the only other person to attend to the body was Doctor Hobart.

"What do you make of it, Doc?"

"Could be a heart attack."

The sheriff leaned the full weight of his body into the tire tracks and peered closely. "I don't think so. Look right here." His hand followed the skid marks away from the mangled truck and back to the street. "Lost control." The doctor nodded though not convinced of the analysis. Why did he ask his opinion if he had already formed his own? The sheriff gestured for him to follow. "Looks to me like he took the turn a little too hard."

"But what do you make of his body slumped over the steering wheel like it was?"

The sheriff paused and pulled his hat up with contemplation. "Impact."

"With the speedometer stuck at 25, he wasn't speeding."

"27."

The doctor frowned. "What I'm saying is that we can't rule out some medical reason for the crash. And until we get an autopsy report…"

"Listen, Doc, seems to me that you so called "medical experts" are always lookin' for some reason for this or that even when the answer is starin' ya straight in the face. Rain makes mud that makes for slippery roads. Elementary school science; he swerved right into the tree. And that's what we're gonna write in the accident report. Now if you excuse me." The sheriff moseyed over to the patrol car and got in.

A circle of bystanders had been dispersed earlier though several loitered about even after they were instructed to go home. Three boys on bikes flanked the road.

"Any of you fellahs see the accident?"

They turned to each other waiting for the largest boy to speak. "We were over there when we heard the crash," he exclaimed pointing across the road. "It sure as shit was loud."

"But none of you saw anything?"

"You a cop, cause ya don't look like a cop."

"No, I'm Doctor Hobart."

The boy winked at the others and leaned over the handlebars. "Then I bet you seen the body?" he hinted with macabre interest. The others pitched forward hoping too to hear some of the gory details.

The doctor shook his head, no, and like disappointed birds at an empty feeder, they rode away. The annoyed physician had lied. He did see the body, but it had been strangely serene; almost as though Fairbanks had been dead before the crash.

———

The gray man felt no remorse over the death of JJ, but he did feel sorry when he heard about Jen. He and the mother had shared a few good times, but he didn't feel compelled to call on the woman. It would only stir up a lot of unpleasant emotions that needed to remain unstirred. He laughed at the thought of the Preacher coming between him and the woman. Though he couldn't really blame her, he was a smooth son-of-a-bitch. She was prickly on the outside but vulnerable to a man who professed he could give her comfort; even if it was disguised as salvation.

He pierced the top of the can and let the beer flow into the glass. He would have rather been at the bar but was too lazy to go out; it seemed more trouble than it was worth. The foam drew up above the rim and he waited as it began to settle down. The first mouthful was always the best. Salvation; that was something only the Preacher could provide her with. How could he have competed with that? He guzzled the beer and set it down hard on the coffee table.

He poured the remaining contents and listened to the foam swelling and rising; creating the only divide between the drinker and his beer. From his chair he could see the leash was still on the floor right where it had dropped. He missed the dog; it was a good companion. But now he felt betrayed. Like the woman, he had been good to it, only to be let down. As far as he was concerned, he was giving up on women. But as for dogs, he would have to think about that. He finished the beer and picked up the leash. He stretched it across on the table. For another dollar he could have had a name stamped into the leather, but he was too cheap. He coiled it up and tossed it into a box of newspapers. He wouldn't throw it away just yet.

All that day he questioned the whereabouts of the dog and by nightfall he was fatigued by his contemplations. He was not the philosophical type but every now and again he would compare one situation with another. With the dog he was not sensing a loss but more of a failure. His father always reminded him what a failure he had been. He was sure that when he returned home from his stint in the army he would finally have lived up to the old man's standards, but it was too late. He was buried before his son's return.

The grayness of the evening melted into his mood. He felt hungry. There was a TV dinner in the freezer, a beer in the fridge, and boxing on television. The dog always slept on the rug when he watched television. It would stretch out across the whole half of the floor and he would have to step over it to get into the kitchen. It was an enormous obstruction, taking up much more space than it needed. The gray man thought about the dog and wondered what it was eating for dinner.

A loud and impetuous knock on the door came as an intrusion. He thought for a moment of not answering it, but decided against it when it came again, this time with more urgency.

Gil Adler was standing before the entranceway.

"You drunk?"

"No, not yet.

The gray man turned and led him into the living room. He returned from the kitchen with two cans. "Here."

"I guess you're wondering why I'm here." He stood nervously taking several long slugs and then wiped his mouth on his sleeve.

"You look like shit."

"Thanks." He smiled meekly. "I need to sort out a problem. It's just that I can't remember if I saw something the other night or if it was a dream."

The gray man nodded, "And?"

"And, if I wasn't dreaming then I saw a dead body and if I am dreaming then I saw a dead body."

"When did this happen?"

"That's part of the problem. I don't know."

The gray man switched on the television and sat down. "Want to watch the fights?"

"I think I saw a dead woman."

The indifferent host turned and looked into troubled eyes. "I wouldn't worry about a dead woman, it's the ones that are alive that you need to worry about."

Nineteen

THE LIST, HOMEWARD, AND A HISTORY LESSON

D r. Hobart removed the pen from out of the desk drawer and added two more names to his list: Doug Fairbanks and Jen. The plain town had buried two more of its own. The autopsy reports had not come back and even though he had related his concerns to the authorities, each case was being treated as an isolated incident. The notion that Jen had died of a broken heart was the most ridiculous rubbish he had ever heard, yet those who attended church that Sunday were reminded of the powers of a distraught heart. As far as the townsfolks were concerned, they were divided in two beliefs; those who claimed it was all part of the Lord's big plan and those who say she was taken too soon.

Misery rose out of the hills and into the church like it was on fire. It fell over the mother and the sisters with a vengeance. The mother's thoughts caressed the image of despair while she began to put herself on trial. It was a sad and pitiful sight and not a syllable was spared as the mourners of the plain town came to pay their respects. Enveloped in the recollections of the past and struggling with the present, they tried to console each other, but with little coercion relapsed into their private silence of hardship. When the service was all over, they were led to the cemetery where an ermine-white casket was lowered into the ground. Afterwards, everyone was invited back to the rectory for cake.

Gil Adler tossed a daisy he had picked up off the neighboring tombstone into the open grave. The wind rustled and a dove moaned. "There was nothing I could do for you," he whispered and waited for an instant as though expecting an answer. "You know how I get when I drink, why I thought it was a dream." He sat down by the edge of the hole and leaned in. "You sure got a lot of nice flowers. Why right over here is a big ring of them, biggest wreath I ever saw, except maybe on Christmas." He shifted his feet and unloosed some dirt. It rolled down and landed on top of the casket. "Nothin' I could do for ya," he repeated as he wiped the remorse from his eyes. He put his hand to his brow and looked out across the cemetery as if he were an early settler. "What the hell!" he cried. In throwing distance from the gravesite was the yellow dog. It stopped and wagged its tail and then trotted over to him. "Everywhere I go I see you! You, you damn dog!"

The dog did not seem fazed by the man's lack of affection and simply licked his hand and romped away.

The man was stunned by the dog's gesture. He dried his hand on his pant leg. "That dog is nothin' but a nuisance," he told the dead woman. His feet unsettled more earth and the loose soil rolled again down into the hole producing several hollow thuds as if it were falling hail.

A shadow came between him and the sunlight parting his thoughts away from the dog. "You better get on along now, fellah."

"It's time, huh?"

A man with a shovel was standing over him. "Want to get this closed up now. You go on home." He waited as the seated man fumbled and then raised himself up. "You okay, mister?"

"Yeah, I'm okay." Gil Adler stepped away and watched as the younger man scooped up a shovelful of dirt and pitched it into the hole. He waited while two more were tossed. Then he stepped forward and peered in.

"Bout how many?"

The man with the shovel stopped and balanced it against his shoe. "How many what?"

"How many shovels 'til it's full?"

The man with the spade scratched his chin. "Don't know."

"What do ya mean ya don't know!"

"That's what I said, I don't know!"

"How can you not know?"

"Cause I never counted." He scooped up another shovelful of dirt and tossed it into the grave.

"That's four." Gil Adler brought up four fingers.

"Four. You want to make this sweet?"

Gil looked more interested. "What's ya got in mind?"

"How 'bout we make a wager. Each of us can guess how many shovelfuls and the one that's closest gets the money."

It took only a few moments for the wager to be sealed with a handshake. "What if we're both really wrong, like way off?"

"It's like horseshoes. The closest number wins."

"Got to be the same amount of dirt on the shovel each time."

The shoveler nodded in agreement, "That's fair."

The gravedigger turned to the mound of dirt and sifted through it until he found a rock. Then he set it aside and each man placed ten dollars under it. The man with the shovel counted each time he tossed the dirt and Gil Adler would make a mark with a stick in the bare earth. The hole was about half-way filled when a mustached fellow in a tweed suit and black patent leather shoes hurried over. He was breathing heavily as though he was not used to walking quickly. "We have to close the front gate; so I am afraid that you will have to leave."

"Who me?"

The man with the shovel kept working except now with a quickened pace. "I told him that 'bout an hour ago, but he insisted that he wait around 'til it was all filled in." He grunted and tossed another shovelful.

Gil Adler looked about rather perplexed. He eyed his money and then eyed both men.

"Sorry for your loss, mister, but we must be closing the gates. It's getting late; I am sure you understand."

The shoveler didn't look up, but kept working.

The suited man put his arm around Gil and gave him a nudge of encouragement. "Here, let me walk you out. I understand what a difficult time this must be for you."

The dirt fell swiftly over the coffin and after each toss there sounded a grunt. The reluctant mourner twisted his head round in hopes of getting the attention of the worker. However, the attention he wished for was not the one he received, for as he was led him away he saw the shoveler toss him a wink and stash both of the tens in his pocket.

"Such a loss," the mustached man sighed. "Such a loss."

"You don't know the half of it," agreed Gil Adler.

————

"When a virus undergoes gradual mutation, a new subtype can emerge, increasing its capability of infecting a completely different animal species." Matthew Kamer scribbled the note on the bottom of his lecture

sheet. He tapped his pencil against the desk and added; *"When an animal is infected with two different strains at the same time, the genetic material of the viruses may mix to produce a new strain which contains some of the characteristics of both."* This he underlined. Tomorrow he was scheduled to arrive home for a brief respite before heading back on the road. He was aware of the importance of his lecture series to his career; however, he was also aware of the time it was taking away from his.... He thought for a moment and looked about anxiously striving to fill in the blank when a feeling of profound sadness completed his thought. It was taking away from his life.

He had already proved the new vaccine had positive effects, yet if his most recent hypothesis was correct, there could be adverse implications; inferring the results of the first trials might be flawed. He leaned his head back and rehashed his argument against these suspicions. *"Birds and mammals have different glycan receptors, which creates a natural barrier and prevents the viruses from easily spreading between humans and animals.* So why am I still having misgivings?" His conflicting thoughts drifted around in his head and he sighed, noting that he was hungry. He gathered the loose papers and stacked them neatly before placing them back into his briefcase. A grease-stained hotel menu was the object of his attention, and he perused the dinner column until he eyed the roasted chicken. He glanced across the room checking the clock; and though he may be the first one in the dining room, he decided it was time to eat.

A tall and lean man in his early fifties stood behind the podium. "Good evening, Sir," he yawned. His mouth was too wide for his face.

"Table for one," said the scientist.

"One." The maître d' held up a menu and gestured for him to follow. He stopped at a small table by the window and pulled out the chair. "Miss Banger will be your waitress."

"Banker?"

"No, Banger. Like bang but with an er at the end. Banger."

Kamer repeated, "Banger."

The man grinned and slithered away.

Kamer began to read the menu even though he knew what he wanted when after a few minutes a short but well-provisioned woman approached. "Hello, I'm Ethel, your waitress. Do you need a few more minutes?"

He looked up and smiled. "Big head," he thought.

She stared at him as though she had read his mind. "The sliced head of lettuce salad is very good, one of the specialties of the house."

He took a sip of water and cleared his throat. "Sounds good," he agreed halfheartedly.

She scribbled the salad order on her pad and dabbed the pencil tip with her tongue. "The bigmouth bass is also quite good. Comes with baby potatoes."

"Bass, bass," he repeated. He needed a moment to think, but she had already added it to the pad.

"I'll put your order right in. Be right back with more water." She retrieved the menu and lumbered away.

Annoyed that he had not ordered the chicken, he placed his napkin on his lap and glanced around the room. As predicted, he was the sole diner. Another waiter leaned against the wall with an attentive eye on the entrance. A barely audible song was playing in the background, which would not have been noticed had there been more conversations going on.

Retreating from the kitchen, the waitress reappeared with a basket of breadsticks, a dish of chipped ice lined with several pats of butter, and ice water. She lifted the pitcher and let it flow into the already too full glass. "I'll go check on your salad," she said and scurried away like an escaping rabbit.

Kamer pulled the basket towards him, fingered the breadstick, and placed one on the small bread plate. It was too long and hung over the sides uncomfortably; so he broke it in half and quickly dusted the crumbs to the side. He was used to eating alone, but this evening was particularly disagreeable. He wasn't sure if it was the large-headed waitress, the fact that he didn't really like freshwater fish, or if he was just ready to go home. A sense of weariness overcame his desire to eat. He picked up the breadstick and stabbed it in the butter before taking a bite. Then he chastised himself remembering that he needed to be careful biting into hard food; his teeth were not as reliable as they used to be.

Miss Banger returned balancing an unwieldy tray and placed his salad before him. "I always put the dressing on the side," she remarked. "Be right back with the rest of your order."

He pulled the wedge apart with his fork and poured what appeared to be a creamy ranch dressing. He shredded it into pieces and again wondered if the waitress knew her head was big. Had she suggested the bass regarding his silent reference to the oversized-mouth of the maître d'? He glanced around the room hoping that some others may come in to dine while he was placing his order; however, the only distraction was the rearranging of the menus by the maître d' at his station.

As if in perfect harmony to his last bite of salad, the bass appeared just as he had set the fork down on the empty plate. "It's hot, so be careful," the waitress warned as if he were a small boy and not a grown man.

Kamer looked at the fish and it stared back. He blinked, the fish did not. "That's good," he thought and with a bit of contention he picked up his knife and picked at it. The tip of the blade tore the skin, splitting it apart effortlessly. A distinctive smell of garlic and bait pierced his senses and he winced.

"Hope it's good," declared a voice from behind. Kamer glanced up at a cynical face forging a smile. "If I were you," whispered the loitering waiter as he bent his head towards the diner's ear, "I would have ordered the chicken."

———

The plain town was not noted for anything in particular. It wasn't a place that had much to display nor did it harbor anything that was remarkably ill-suited. It was ordinary; but like a ripe banana, if you peeled back the skin it had more to offer than what was on the outside. The plain town bears a layer of history that it wears without pretense. And although it does not appear to have a remarkable nor prestigious pedigree, its residents come from a strong and determined collection of founders. Stored in the basement of the city hall's archives are ledgers of historical records. One particular narrative, seldom dusted off, recounts the unofficially named "Rebellion of 1896"; an ambitious and rather bravado uprising by a disgruntled group of farmers and their leader, Jacob Albert Adams. Claiming to be a distant relative of the late President John Quincy Adams, Jacob was a struggling farmer and like many others in his day believed he was being unfairly over-taxed. While he may be just a footnote in history, his audacious attempt to assassinate the Governor and seize the Capital with his angry mob of dissidents came as a complete shock to most of the locals. And he just may have been successful had his plan not been unintentionally foiled by his wife, Kitty.

Kitty Walker was the only daughter of a wealthy landowner from Canada. After a brief courtship by Jacob, he brought her to the United States where they traveled the country looking for the best and cheapest land, finally settling down on the outskirts of town. Though her marriage to Jacob was met with disapproval by her father who was not pleased that she was determined to marry an American; the young Adams had all the makings of a good husband. But, he was a farmer with political ambitions, which mixed as well as sprinkling seeds with ocean water.

Unlikely as it seemed, the plain town proved to be a "Fertile Crescent" attracting other folks who also harbored resentment towards the state's tax practices. With Jacob's notoriety as a fair man, possessed by nerve and ambition, he was elected the leader of an underground group calling themselves the *Farmers Against Over-Taxation*. And though not against taxes in general, they were wholeheartedly against what they deemed unfair practices.

For over a year it was as if the coalition were buried beneath the ground. Secret meetings around the neighboring towns and counties consumed the lives of the discontent. Support had grown to an unprecedented size with over 100 farmers and businessmen joining the ranks. But what to do with this unfettered mass of energy was becoming a dilemma. While the plain town's popular leader was prospering in notoriety, Adams's followers were growing restless and now demanded that he advance with a plan lest they lose momentum.

It was a quiet afternoon; the snow fell lightly and the land accepted this blanket of white like a coverlet on an unquilted bed. Jacob and ten prominent members had already departed for the Capital. During the same week others from around the state followed and situated themselves nearby as the rebellion's hour drew near. On the morning of the revolt the snow continued to mount. Extra workers were deployed to clear the streets and shovel the steps of the Capital Building as the dissenters awaited instructions. But what was not known on this day of impending revolution was the accidental interception of a note. During this inclement weather the letter had slipped out of the postman's sack and fallen facedown into the snow. The penned address smeared exposing an ink-stained blemish on the parchment envelope. But as fate steered the day, the reliable postman retrieved it from the wet sidewalk, and seeing that in its illegible condition could not be delivered, he took upon himself to open it up in hopes of finding a clue to the recipient's address.

The pealing of the noontime church bells sounded with the zealous outcries of unruly voices. Adams, at the head of his brigade, was the first to reach the double doors; and once they were breached he prompted the others to follow. Unfamiliar with a room of such size and opulence, it intimidated some while for others it only fueled their anger. It was a room dimly lit by gilded sconces casting murky shadows that stained their cold cheeks. But in contrast to the frigid outdoors, the warmth of the interior quickly stoked their resolve. Some forged left, some right, but those who followed Adams ascended the stairs with heavy and determined strides towards the Governor's office.

And though the narration of this event may have elongated the time the renegades had taken over the Capital, it was in truth less than ten minutes. The "good-luck" note by their leader's wife, Kitty, was the very one rescued by the postman and rerouted to the Governor prior to the insurgence. Within its pithy statement and sweet sentiments, it unwittingly revealed their plot. And depending upon one's position in the plain town, the finders of this historical document may or may not have been pleased with the outcome. The Governor had been secretly escorted to safety through the back exit while the farmers were handily carted away before a single hair on the elder statesman's silver head could be mussed.

Twenty

THE BARBERSHOP, THE DINER, AND
THE HOUSE ON THE HILL

No one saw the yellow dog, but he was watching from across the street. The rain pelted the shop window. "Closed" was all that the sign read. It was handwritten in large and bold letters. The dead barber's brother taped it to the inside of the window. Most everyone by this time knew about the death although there were a few hopefuls that tried the door handle. They jiggled the knob a few times just to be sure, and walked away with the sudden reminder of what had happened. The dog kept his eyes on the gray man as he approached the locked door. It wagged its tail as his owner dipped beneath the rain-dripped awning. Finding it locked, the man turned away and jogged down the street. The dog did not follow; it had too much sense to move from its shelter beneath the bus bench. The rain continued to slam the pavement. He watched as the gray man ducked inside a doorway and then disappeared into the pharmacy.

The number 6 expelled a long sigh and came to an abrupt stop. It was a minute early. The driver opened the doors and peered out while a steady stream of passengers descended. Each stopped by the doorway before exiting and fumbled with their umbrellas. The driver looked at his watch as the line extended back to the middle of the bus. "Rain," grimaced a woman who awaited her turn.

The driver nodded with disapproval.

"Good for the plants or if you're a duck." There was a chorus of chuckles at the woman's attempt at displacing any ill feelings for the day.

The final passenger had barely stepped onto the curb when the door creaked shut and the bus veered away. The windshield wipers tossed the water onto the street.

The dog tucked its feet towards its head when a pair of legs now blocked its view. Above him sat Gil Adler wearing a paper hat and tattered raincoat. He was the only passenger who did not have an umbrella or a destination. The dog lay its head down and inadvertently nudged the seater's leg. The wet man bent down to see what had hit him and noticed the dog.

"So, it's you!" he exclaimed.

The dog shifted back.

"Seems like we always meet, don't we!" His breath smelled of day-old liquor. "Don't be afraid, I just came to say hello."

Finding the voice not a threat, it licked the hand that was now wiggling before his nose.

"Ugh, what'd you that for?" The hand drew back, and he wiped it on his coat.

The dog remained still and waited. Like most things that came Gil's way, he knew it would eventually leave. He sat while his hat absorbed too much water and finally collapsed. He could feel his wet hair droop down below his ears. He removed the newspaper and rolled it into a ball. He shoved it into his coat pocket, leaned over the side of the bench, and looked beneath the seat. "Well, so long now, pooch."

Gil Adler started across the street. He wiped his hand across his forehead and continued towards the barbershop. He split the rain as he walked and the grayness fell over him. He reached for the door. It was locked. He tried again, but his effort was useless.

The dog opened its eyes and watched as the wet man cupped his hands round the window and peered in. It saw him turn away, however, contrary to the gray man this one did not run, but walked somberly in the opposite direction.

Unlike the others in the plain town, Gil Adler had little recollection of why the barbershop would be closed. He shrugged his shoulders trying to conjure up a reason. As far as he remembered it wasn't a holiday, it wasn't Sunday or Monday, and it was daylight. He moved along in the rain like a corpse. The cars that passed paid little heed. Their tires splattered mud and water up onto the sidewalk. He thought he was cold but that feeling soon passed. The rain was compassionless. He tried to recollect where he had slept for he did not remember getting dressed this morning. He was losing days. Events he remembered were relegated to long ago whispers in his thoughts. His feet moved without the direction of his head. He shivered, stopped, and then looked down. A slip of paper adhered to the sidewalk and he peeled it up. It began to rip so he crouched down and cocked his head to the side to read it. "Revival Meeting." The Preacher was resurrected. He stood up and mashed the flyer with his foot. It was a ball of pulp beneath his shoe. He scraped his sole against the curb and grinded down harder until the final bits of paper were freed. They fell into the gutter and drifted effortlessly with the rainwater.

"Shit!" He heaved a sigh and carried the Preacher with him as he started along on his walk. The wind tousled his hair and the liquor tousled his thoughts. Together they muddled his clarity. The Preacher came and went uninvited like when he was younger. Only in his youth he could close the door or leave when the Bible thumper came round. His mother would place the house key under the geranium planter. He always could tell without going inside when Lloyd Tritch was visiting. The key would be missing.

The walk to the river was thick with mud and the weight of the Preacher made his journey difficult. The slick trail slipped easily beneath his feet. A few times he lost his footing and when he fell he tried to free himself of his burden. But it remained intact. On a sunny day the path to the riverbank was carefree. But on this ash and slate colored day, the Preacher too had decided to come along. Gil Adler stopped and stretched. It was too quiet now. The Preacher lay heavily but even in the rain the religious man's face appeared bright. Gil wondered if anyone saw him and stirred around like a frightened chipmunk. But his feet dared not go any farther. With the load bearing its full weight upon him, he could feel his knees buckle; he could walk no more. The rain was a tireless companion. "If I could just sleep," he groaned. He leaned over, his face peering down on the grassy knoll. He crawled like a dog towards a large oak and stubbed his knee on the gnarled roots. "I feel sick," he complained. The Preacher was no longer with him. "I must have dropped him along the way!" A bank of clouds hovered like a swarm of locust, blackening the sky with fits of thunder. "I think I'm sick," he complained and rested back against the trunk.

"That lazy drunk owes me money!"

"What drunk?"

"Which one do you think?"

Pearl paused. "You mean that poor soul, Gil Adler?"

"Son-of-a-bitch took advantage of my good nature."

"I'm afraid you don't know the meaning of good-natured. Just think of it as charity."

"Screw charity, next time I see that lush I'll be damn sure to get my ten bucks, back! Maybe with interest!"

She pulled the bowl towards her. "Toss a couple oyster crackers on the side will ya, Connie."

The cook frowned, but complied. "You're too damn generous for your own good."

"Only when it comes to makin' tips, sugar." She smiled and sauntered towards the table.

The parking lot was flooded on the east side. Pearl peered out the door at her car and then down at her shoes. The water would surely come up above her ankles. There was a kind of almost cozy feeling inside which kept some of the truckers eating at a more leisurely pace. "This was good," she thought. "The longer they stay, the more tips." The stormy weather did not deter them from coming by. In fact, the harder it poured the more likely their visibility was poor; a good excuse to pull over. It was a domino effect in her favor. The counter bell sounded like an impatient school bell returning her back to work like a child at recess. A steaming bowl of stew was waiting along with Connie's bad attitude.

"Hear that?" he asked.

"Hear what?"

"Shhh! Somethin' at the back door." He stopped to listen.

"Go see, then." Now she was fed up with his lousy mood. A long pitiful whine was caught up in the wind. "Yea, now I do." She scurried into the kitchen and opened the delivery door. A torrent of rain and a wet yellow dog tried to barge in, only to be intercepted by the cook.

"Not so fast!" he bellowed and pushed the dog back outside with his foot.

"But he's cold," wailed the woman.

"Yeah, but there's a little something like a health code."

She knew he was right. "I suppose, poor thing."

"First a drunk, now a wet dog. You're a regular bleeding heart." He slammed the door shut.

For a moment the waitress tossed the idea of sneaking the animal into the bathroom, but thought better of her own allergies. Dog hair and cat hair; both sent her into a sneezing fury. Reversing her sentiment, she agreed, "I suppose you're right."

The day grew and the water rose. With brush strokes of gray ink the rain streaked across the land. The dog shook its fur with little improvement to its condition. It stood for a few minutes like a dejected beggar, which it was. It scampered over to the garbage pails and knocked one over. The can rolled a few feet and generously released the lid. The dog buried his head inside, forging quickly before the water would carry away any of its contents. There were meager pickings, some vegetable peels and sheets of soggy newspaper. The wet dog crept inside. The can resonated, broadcasting the pelting drops against the tin with thundering vibrations. It backed out dragging with it something raw. The back door flung open; a series of expletives were carried away by the wind. It looked up and bolted down the alley with its stingy find dangling from its mouth.

———

It finally stopped raining by the time the dog reached the white house on the top of the hill. Along the way it rested under the hawthorn tree. The brooding canopy sheltered him from the open road. He swallowed the raw meat and then threw it up whole. He sniffed it and walked away. The dog was several yards from the tree when he heard a shadow fluttering between the branches, the caw of a scavenger. The bird swooped down, scouted the area, and flew overhead with the raw meat until it could not be seen.

There was a car in the garage but the dog didn't know that because the door was padlocked. None of the lights were on inside, only the porch light had been left attracting moths from the evening before. The dog stood by the shed, nudged the door, but it too was locked. He sniffed the air, then the ground, and sneezed. A sprinkle of water was dislodged. He looked up at the house. The last flow of water was wearily draining from the gutter spouts, fated to catch up with a muddy stream heading downhill. The dog scampered over to the gravesite. The water droplets captured the sunlight, and the headstone was given an iridescent patina. The yellow dog walked over Mrs. Kamer and found the area it liked best. During the rains the holes had refilled with mud. The dog noised around, pushed against the soft earth and began to dig. It unsealed the muddy film like a jar of jelly and kicked up muck behind him. The burden of the water had loosened the ground and cleansed the sky.

Dr. Kamer was eating a pimento cheese sandwich. He felt a slight tingle on his cheeks; a prickly sensation caused by the olives which always turned his usual pallor complexion rosy. The bottle of milk sat on the table, and he took a swig. This was a new habit he acquired since living alone. He placed it back on the table and peered up towards the ceiling. "Sorry," he apologized and then took another bite of the sandwich. A small pile of newspapers had accumulated on the porch. He had forgotten to tell the Haddon boy not to deliver when he was away. Most had been badly soaked by the rain. The ink ran, bleeding the words together like a gray cloud.

But there were a few days' worth that could be salvaged and these he had laid out on the kitchen counter to dry.

A great deal of what happened in the plain town was driven on needs and instinct making the world effectually controlled by those who lived outside its perimeter. As such, it didn't generate much news to stoke the imagination or change the course of daily events, but reading the local paper during breakfast had been a routine that he did not wish to retire. Directly after his lunch he would go outside and let Matilda know he was home. He wasn't a religious or superstitious man, but just in case, he didn't want her to think he didn't care. He sighed and his chest heaved as he stood up to rinse the dishes. The drying newspaper was beginning to curl up at the corners. He reached over and then placed the salt and pepper shakers and mustard container on top of the creeping edges. With a light brush of his hand he stroked the seam when a headline caught his eye. "Multiple Deaths Leaves Town in Mourning."

"Multiple?" He leaned into the paper and began to read the article. "The long list of deceased is considered a rare but unfortunate coincidence." He fingered the names and then stopped at Doug Fairbanks. "Why he was just here not but a few months ago." He walked over to the sink and poured a glass of water. No sooner had he turned the handle then did it resonate with a heightened reminder of the dead plumber. "Well, this certainly is some news. I better let Matilda know."

The day was beginning to show itself differently than usual. He ruminated about his own few weeks filled with self-acknowledgement and testimony to his hard work. A contented grin fell over his lips. A sense of accomplishment is something that cannot be bought, but rather must be earned. Yet, at what price? This was the undisclosed moment of truth that only he could share with his wife. "She was my Madame Curie and I was her Pierre. Well, maybe I am being melodramatic," he thought half-jesting. "But she certainly did her part for me. Maybe she wasn't schooled in the sciences, but she was my trusted assistant nevertheless." He smiled as he summoned up her image. He pushed the chair away from the table and dusted the few crumbs with his hand onto the floor. He looked down and scooted them with his shoe across the linoleum. Another habit he had acquired while being alone.

Outside the dog sniffed feverishly and settled upon a fresh mound of softened earth. Its excavations remained a secret, hidden in the platitude of Kamer's ignorance. The clouds circled above lassoing the sun, keeping it from heating the ground. The yellow dog did not tire from his work. Only the body and wagging tail could be seen for the head and ears were obscured. His front paws worked the ground, scratching, separating, draining the hole of its contents. And as he pushed his nose he could smell the damp ground, beating the earth with his determination until finally rewarded. It lifted its head and snorted. His foot pawed inside the cavity and the sides crumbled revealing the purpose of his interest. The clouds parted and the sun entered the hole delivering to the dog its stash. He gnawed at the muddied piece of muslin until he was able to grasp it between his front teeth. His first attempt to dislodge it from the earth was met with little measure. It tore as easily as if it had been cut with scissors. The sheltered object remained seemingly intact, wrapped securely within its cloth cocoon.

Kamer piled his dishes into the sink alongside the other dirty plates and cups and for a fleeting moment chastised his procrastination towards housework. With the intention of making amends, he ran some water into the sink and reconciled with his disappointed-self that he would wash them later. The absolved man had an appointment and unapologetic, he opened the back door while reaching into his empty trouser pockets. "What did I do with them?" he mumbled. With hopes of stirring a quick recollection, he went into the living room, but among the forces that were able to outwit the scientist was his uncanny ability to misplace his keys.

The room seemed more cluttered than usual as he looked around, tossing aside the TV guide laying open on the coffee table and reaching between the sofa cushions. He scoured beneath the armchair and then lumbered back into the kitchen where he lifted his jacket off the counter. The car keys fell out of the pocket, revealing both the hiding place and a reminder of his absent mindedness. A fleeting thought of Matilda circulated for a moment, but this hesitation was arrested with the reminder of his meeting. Without delay or knowledge of the dog in his yard, he opened the door and went directly to the garage in anticipation of driving to Doctor Hobart's.

The dog stood by the hole and watched as the man rumbled down the driveway. The cloth had given way, unmasking several glass cylinders. The dog licked and licked as he tried to stretch its tongue into the cavity of the smallest one. It licked all four clean and then picked up the largest in its mouth and carried it over to the shed. The sun shined brilliantly. He was hot and thirsty. He toppled the watering can that had collected rain and drank from the pool that had spilled. The cylinder rolled into the puddle and remained submerged until some of the water was absorbed by the saturated land and reached its level. The dog laid down in the puddle stretching out in the shade. The dry mud slowly loosened and dropped from his fur and from between the pads on his paws. He licked his feet. He was hungry but was too tired and content to scavenge. The wind rolled the cylinder and it rattled with an unfamiliar sound. He opened his eyes and saw the cylinder as it became settled next to a rock. The sunlight hit the glass and a kaleidoscope of colors appeared. The dog sighed, licked his chops, and trotted back to the hole for more.

———

When the station wagon pulled up to the garage the dog was gone. Kamer kept the engine running as he stepped out of the car and around to the front. With a more than usual amount of effort he pulled the door open, got back behind the wheel, and drove in. The smell of oil and gasoline permeated the building. He leaned his head on the steering wheel and for a few moments lapsed into a short-lived sense of peace. The notion of driving again sent his head into an immediate ache. He looked at his watch and putting aside the idea of his upcoming trip, he began sorting through mental notes of the past few hours. He transcribed his conversation about Doug Fairbanks. All those unresolved questions about the dead man had given rise to the doctor's curiosity. He was flattered that the physician believed he might be able to shed some light on the cause of death. *"Well, that's why I called you. Seems like the lab came up short. As far as they can tell he was infected with something, a virus they can't identify."* Kamer mulled the exchange over in his mind. Furnished with a complete report he might be able to formulate a better analysis. He slammed the car door and hurried towards the little gravesite.

———

The house on the hill was white, a ghostly image forged against the pale sky. The rain had splattered mud against the clapboards, speckled brown as though having been deliberately thrown. That was a long time ago when he heaved dirt bombs at toy soldiers. It was a harmless game of war far away from the real death and devastation. It was easy to make trenches in the garden; deep enough to conceal an infantry. But they were not able to withstand the air attack and crumbled mercilessly beneath an assault of mud bombs. *"What the hell is going on!"* his mother's voice penetrated his memory of whitewashing the stained boards, but now translated into the present, he heard his own voice cry out; "what the hell is going on!"

A hollow trail of dog tracks circled the marble headstone. A nose print of dirt slid from the top to the bottom. Throwing his arms up in disbelief, he hurried to the site and tapped the disturbed earth with his shoe and then bent down and patted it gently as if tucking in a bedsheet. "Sorry, Matilda." He followed the pawprints, but they were helter-skelter in all directions leading to the presumption that they had been delivered over a period of several hours. A few meters away the ground had been molested and holes of various sizes had been excavated. He stopped and peered over the disturbed site. A cool breeze brought to life the sleeping earth. "Shit!" Kamer felt his mouth go dry. "Shit!" The pattern of scratches, the lifted dirt that had remained dormant now awakened undisturbed memories. He leaned down and collided with reality. Like a breath beneath the earth, the buried objects had been expelled.

That dog, the yellow dog. Kamer frowned. Taking a quick lap around the garden he headed to the shed to retrieve gloves and the rake.

"Rinse these well, Mattie."

"I will dear." Her smile melted away as he picked about the ground. Like salt in an open wound the discovery of missing

glassware stung. He raked the area and stamped down. The damp earth was wonderfully soft. He raked over and over, making a thin track of grooves.

"*Make sure its deep. Don't want any vermin to uncover it.*" His mother had directed the funeral arrangements of all the deceased pets. Several guinea pigs and a hamster had been interred before he reached the age of seven. "*Rake it over, and be careful not to upset what you already done! Rake it real fine, fine smooth lines. Matthew, you hear what I said, slower.*"

Kamer raked more slowly. Then he wondered what happened to the buried sacks; and the dog, that damn dog.

––––––

As if knowing it was carrying something of value, the yellow dog never released the last sack he had uncovered. It dangled from his mouth jiggling the glass within its contents. A light tinkling like wind chimes sounded free from within the bag. And when the dog stopped, so did the clinking.

He must have been quite a sight trotting along the road. With unrestrained instinct he exploited each moment to his advantage. The rains never deterred the hound, but rather cleared the streets and roads for his comings and goings. It rather enjoyed the mud for it cooled him like swine in the sty. If he missed the gray man it did not let on, for as smart as the dog was, it never seemed to find its way back home.

Twenty-One

THE GRAY MAN, THE PREACHER, AND KAMER

Pearl's vitality stemmed from her youthful spirit. She was tired of interchanging Pearl with Juanita and though the latter received a goodly amount of well-deserved attention, she found that the unsophisticated customers always needed her to pronounce the name correctly. However, the decision to replace it was a flimsy excuse when the fact was she was really poetically capricious. To assume a surrogate personality was altogether quite easy. After pouring her first cup of coffee, she closed her eyes, circled her finger in the air, and then placed it randomly upon the wall map as if playing pin-the-tail on the donkey. When she opened her eyes she found it had landed squarely on California. She smiled with the prospect; so many choices, so many good choices; but after a moment's deliberation decided to adopt the name from "the First Lady of American Cinema", the one and only Lillian Gish. Besides, Lillian should not trip up the tongue of anyone in the plain town.

———

The gray man peered over his glasses at the photograph. He picked up the framed picture and thought, "That's a great dog." Fearing he might be getting sentimental, he set it face down on the shelf, but it was too late; the photo was colored with nostalgia and he couldn't help but feel a bit regretful. He had put a lot of energy into the dog and had grown quite fond of the animal. It had become a positive distraction in his not so positive life. He reached for the photograph again and wiped the glass with his shirttail. "Where the hell are you?" He replaced the frame right-side up and pushed it away from the shelf's edge.

Last night's poker game netted a loss of a little more than ten dollars. He hadn't intended to play. The bar was always busy on Friday nights; a few beers into the evening and after some friendly conversation he agreed. It wasn't so much losing the money; it was his lousy luck. Nothing was going his way. There was something absent, something missing. The gray man got back into bed. "Gil Adler, yeah, that's what was missing. Wonder where the son-of-a-bitch went off to?"

He had become bored with his life, with the plain town, and his ordinary habits. He glanced over at the photograph. The yellow dog was a companion that didn't take up too much space. They had developed a relationship of understanding; like a friend that you don't have to explain yourself to. But he had given it way too much concern and now it was time for the mutt to come home. He knew that he had not hurt the animal in any way, and so cause for it to be afraid was out of the question. Perhaps it was too much like a man; maybe it possessed a restless quality. Perhaps this dog resembled the kind of man that didn't like to settle down, one that couldn't help the way it was, but needed freedom to go when and where it pleased.

The gray man sat up and noted the hour. He would make some coffee and toast a couple pieces of bread. After breakfast he would set out and find the dog. It was time it came home.

———

Heat levitated above the horizon like a blurry smudge. Behind it was a flat cloudless backdrop, an anemic blue that quivered over the sticky tar road. This was a lucent passage that had all the makings of peeling back like a postage stamp, a mirage capable of lifting and warping on its own as it baked in the sun. And if the edge did curl it would uncover a white void, a place that neither has an end or a beginning; only the vapors of a hot day.

The dog walked on the dirt path. It paralleled the road and a field of green; greens of a forest and the greens of malachite. Dried dandelions and thorny thistles broke the monotony of all the green. The yellow dog was thirsty, but he did not stop to lap up the water heating in the puddles. He trotted in and over them wetting his dry paws. His head drooped under the weight of the sack he held firm. A long thread of saliva dangled freely. Several cars must have noticed the dog as they sped past, most driving over the speed limit except for one rattletrap of a truck with an open-bed filled with chicken coops. The dog stopped as the old clunker steered past. The smell of poultry and manure filled his nostrils and slowly dissipated behind the truck as it rattled down the road.

The dog cowered behind several parked cars as it entered the alley where two garbage cans were aligned. He dropped the sack and nudged his snout along the lid of the first can. Pushing up with his nose, he forced the lid to rise and with very little effort it toppled to the ground. As it gave way to the fall, it produced a sensational clamor, however, within the confines of the diner the disturbance remained unnoticed. The yellow dog now had an easy access to the contents and stuck its head into the filthy cavern, forgetting about the sack it had carried all the way from the white house on the hill.

Several hearty gusts of wind rolled the toppled garbage pail into the parking lot. Potato peels, tomato slices, napkins, and plate scrapings were scattered like confetti. A congress of crows feasted greedily, making a relay back and forth for several minutes until the mishap was discovered by an unhappy patron wearing mashed potato on his boot heel. The birds were scared away and the dog was nowhere in sight.

"I don't know why you didn't let the birds clean it up!"

"Why should I when I have ….," he leaned into her shoulder as he read her latest name, "you, Lillian!"

The waitress wasn't sure if he was kidding. Had it not have been for finding the unusual glassware, she would have had-it-out with the man. But since he agreed that she could set them on the tables; she was satisfied. "You say they were in this filthy sack?" She dangled the bag before him as if displaying day-old catch.

"Yep, out in the alley."

"Kind of funny, don't ya think?" She tossed the bag aside and then wiped the counter with her apron for good-measure.

"I don't know." The cook shrugged his shoulders. "Don't really give a shit."

"Now Connie, don't be so crude!"

"Since when have you become so high and mighty? Hurry up! We got customers to serve!" But within that moment he saw something in the waitress that he may have overlooked and couldn't help but give her credit for trying to be a lady.

Lillian selected four window-tables on which to place the newly found glassware. The bell-shape was a perfect orb to hold water, while the elongated neck supported the gangly wildflowers she picked from across the street.

"You sure have gone to a lot of trouble." The man rounded the tables with a glint of approval. "I suppose it does give the place a bit of...."

"Class?"

"Well, I wouldn't go that far," he laughed and walked towards the men's room.

She stood back and admired her handy-work. She was content with this job, even if she was now the only server. Connie hadn't replaced the dead girl. "A real shame." Her thoughts dwindled to the young waitress and then out into the parking lot and a green truck. It was a dark green pick-up with a bearded driver behind the wheel. He hesitated and then as if changing his mind, made an abrupt U-turn and headed back onto the open road. She watched, quenching her parched curiosity with a daydream. The dark green truck hauling a load, up and over the labyrinth of highways, yet no matter the landscape, the rising sun drying the morning mist or setting in a dusky rain, he will not remember. Not the buds awakening on spring trees nor the full moon flush against the charcoal sky; he will arrive at his destination just like he is now, in a dream. Lillian stowed away with the green pick-up; her thoughts trailing behind the rambling truck until she was reclaimed by a familiar sound of the door opening. She twisted round and a cool breeze entered filling the room with a soft gust followed by Kamer. "Sit anywhere; be right over with a menu." Her friendly greeting across the room was met with a nod.

He walked over to a window-table set for two and pulled out the chair. His eyes penetrated the glass, silent and motionless. He gazed past his own reflection as restless sunlight blotted the table.

"Penny for ya thoughts?" The waitress standing before him challenged his attention. "Haven't seen you in here for a long time, Matt." She smiled at him like a mother smiles at a child.

"Been away; on a lecture series." He slid into the chair and opened the menu as if it were a book of great magnitude that needed to be studied.

"Sounds important. Lecture series." She hesitated for a moment now slightly intrigued by his intelligence. Conversations of relative substance rarely came her way. They were mostly all in fun. Kamer's serious appearance pleased her. "Connie makes a mean meatloaf." Her voice lingered with seduction that came along with her new name.

He glanced quickly at the items and nodded in agreement, not with the suggestion but with the importance of the lecture series.

"One meatloaf comin' right up," she scribbled the order on her pad and snatched the menu away. "Coffee?" She couldn't believe he didn't notice her new name printed on the name tag.

"Yes, sure, coffee." He watched as she sauntered to the back of the diner. It was the second time in less than a week that he ordered something he didn't want.

Unless he was away the scientist rarely ate out; and even if he enjoyed doing so, which he didn't, the plain town offered very few choices. Along Route 10 there was an Italian restaurant, *Bella Luna*, where he and Matilda used to dine on special occasions. They would order a glass of Chianti even though she didn't really enjoy the wine but rather liked the bottle wrapped in jute netting like a pair of mesh stockings. He hadn't been back since her death; it just wouldn't seem right. There was the drugstore with the soda fountain that served lunch. But they closed at three. *Hong's Chinese Restaurant* was wildly popular. It had an atmosphere everyone expected and wanted; plastic lanterns, rice wallpaper printed with scenes of Chinese antiquity, soy sauce paired with hot mustard, and background music offering Oriental ambiance. Just enough authenticity to make you ignore the stained carpet. Other than that, there was the diner.

The scientist tried to show interest in his surroundings and fingered the silverware. He inspected the tongs on his fork, pleased that they appeared to have been adequately washed. He placed his napkin on his lap and smoothed the crinkled paper. It was thinner than the brand of napkins he used at home. He looked outside restlessly and then back to his table setting; concluding that waiting for his meal to be served was the most awkward part of dining out by one's self. Yet this uncomfortable moment was suddenly extinguished, and as if he had been relieved of all blood flow, his face turned a stony white.

"Coffee, Professor?" the waitress interrupted, but his reply was only answered by a morbidly blank expression. "Hey, are you okay?" Lillian asked. "You don't look so good." The coffeepot dangled above his cup as she started to pour.

"Where did you get this?" he exclaimed pointing to the centerpiece.

"Oh, this?" She filled his cup with little regard for the alarmed man's outburst. "Connie found them out back. Kind of different, isn't it?"

"Where, out back?" His mouth was dry as if he were eating sand.

"I don't know; I think by the garbage." And with a simple gesture of her arm he watched it glide from table to table as gracefully as a schooner crosses the sea. Like a dog on a lead, Kamer followed her hand mirror a path along the windowsills. In the center of three tables were identical arrangements of similar glassware.

"Pretty, aren't they?" But by the astonished look on the man's face she wasn't too sure if he agreed.

————

"Now doesn't that take the cake," complained the carping waitress. "He just got up and left without even an explanation."

"Maybe it was something you said. What did you do?"

"Nothin', not a damn thing. I poured him the coffee, and he asked me about the flowers. Then he just stood up and said he had to go."

Connie slid the platter off the counter and dropped the meatloaf back into the pan. "Well, at least you didn't serve this up. All we lost was a cup of coffee."

"No, he paid for that, and left a nice tip too." She patted her pocket.

"Those scientist types are all a little odd."

"I guess," she agreed. "It must have been something about those flowers."

"Well, if it happens again, then they have to go! We can't lose customers 'cause they don't like the flowers, or your new name."

"Don't worry, we won't," she said with a sour turn of her lips and tipping her name tag upward, she pulled it free from her blouse and slipped it into her pocket. "We won't."

————

Kamer scrubbed his hands and then threw the soap and handtowel into the rubbish pail. It didn't seem possible; maybe he had been too hasty in thinking they were the same ones. He closed his eyes and envisioned himself sitting in the diner. But as much as he wished that he had been mistaken, he was quite positive. He had ordered all the labware himself; had picked out each test tube, each vile, each beaker, each flask. No, the volumetric flasks filled with flowers couldn't be a coincidence. The fact that there were three identical ones arranged on other tables only verified his suspicion. They must be the same ones that had been dug up from his yard.

This haunting truth was stealing his day. He turned on the faucet. The water ran clear and cold. He watched as it rushed into the sink and then got sucked into the cavernous drainpipe, violently twisting and turning. He put his hand under the cold stream and let it wash against his flattened palm. It ricocheted off the sink splattering against the sides of the basin and sprayed back into his face and onto his arms. He fumbled with the handle shutting off the water and wiped his eyes with the dishcloth when a horrific thought emerged as if it had burst free from the spigot. Could it be possible that his water was tainted? He hurried as the silent dread led him to the back door and outside. The sun, once overhead, was loitering behind the clouds. It was still oppressively hot. All clarity of reason had been exorcised by his unscientific part of the brain. He reached into his back pocket for his handkerchief and wiped his brow. Then, getting a hold of his composure, he scanned the ground and meandered back inside to the kitchen sink again. He twisted the handle and ran the water and half-filled a drinking glass. He lifted it to the sunlight and shook the glass lightly. A sliver of a rainbow floated on the surface. The troubled man placed the rim to his lips and took a long cool drink. Impossible; he was letting his imagination get the better of him. There was no possible way that the water-table could have been contaminated. If it had been... why he would have been sick long ago.

He sat down at the kitchen table; the place where all big decisions were made and ended. He never really liked the oilcloth table covering, but there were some things in one's life that were better left untouched. The table covering was one of these things. Despite the fact that he was a scientist, he was rather clumsy and had a propensity for not paying attention to little things. Spilling a glass of water or overturning a saltshaker was not uncommon. So it was with the glassware he discovered at the diner. What was done was done. There was nothing he could do about them being used as flower vases. Rather ingenious on the part of Pearl, he thought. Well, if they were now decorations, so be it. It was not his place to bring disharmony to what was nothing more than an innocent mistake on his part. If asked why the hasty retreat from the restaurant, he could explain that the choice of wildflowers could have brought on an immediate attack of hay fever.

Kamer was satisfied with his decision; to simply leave things as they were. His only dissatisfaction was with that dog, that damn dog.

———

The Preacher was drawn to wearing white and in the summer he could satisfy his preference by donning a white suit. The alabaster linen made him feel closer to his "maker", it made him feel that he was a host of the "Heavenly Father", and it especially made him look handsome. It was in the autumn and winter that he was forced to wear clothes of a darker shade, and these he called his "solemn wear".

"I am a man of two seasons even though the good Lord provided us with four." And though the expression is stated as "clothes make the man", he was a firm believer of the contrary. His mood was relegated by the changes in weather and his sermons reflected his altered character. And so, those women that he comforted in the warm months of spring and summer often turned more morose during the colder ones. He remained a creature of habit, enjoying the company of the more fragile gender in overstuffed chairs by fireplaces and woodstoves. But it was during these times that his preaching took on a more revered flavor and those who he guided found him to be less tolerant. In the wintertime, those who sought spiritual guidance at his Sunday revival tent knew that this was not a place for the weak, for in this backwoods church the only warmth delivered was through the spirit of a sermon and not by a heater.

But he was a handsome man; a man who could elevate the non-believers into believing and provide just the right amount of comfort to set them on a righteous path. Still, it was said that in the plain town not everyone liked the Preacher. Maybe they had good reason or maybe it was because they were wearing their winter dispositions.

———

Palling Street is the main road that bisects the plain town from north to south, a straight two-way divide maneuvering both drivers and pedestrians from one end to the other, and vice-versa. Years before the east-west extension was built it was the only way into town; but regardless of the new-improved four lanes that bypasses the traffic, Palling Street continues to be the most favored route. Because of its status as the major artery, most all the old-time residents refer to it as Main Street or just Main for short. Such a habit of calling it by its nickname took hold that in 1933, the town council lobbied to have the name officially changed to Main Street. It all seemed quite logical at the time, an innocent offering to those who were not familiar with its original name by exchanging it with an easier one to remember; seeing as it was indeed "the main street". But this proposal did not come without dissention and when the descendants of the original Palling family challenged the decision with such a grand protest, the effort was deemed unworthy of the trouble. Altering the name was as blasphemous as removing a marker on a gravesite; "Desecrating the honor of our founders," and "a real unpatriotic attempt to supplant their memory."

In 1834, Wilson Wright Palling was the first resident to endorse the town's charter. At first glance he was not a very impressive fellow, rather stumpy with too short legs for his too long arms. But he proved himself no less of a man, making up for his appearance through his honorable character. And though the plain town was never earmarked as having or offering anything of significant importance to his namesakes, it remains inhabited by at least one decedent from the original Palling's. As a founding family their name continues to carry its weight, for never has a Palling been convicted of the slightest of misdemeanors. Four male descendants of Pallings have served as mayors and to date there has always been a Palling on the town council. Noting the stupidity or naiveté of the 1933 council; its residents recognized that to change the name of the street would indeed have been a grave mistake.

Kamer sat at the traffic signal on Palling Street and waited for the light to change. He drummed his fingers against the steering wheel as he watched the gray man cross in front. A young boy and his mother followed behind and as all three stepped up onto the opposite curb the light signaled for him to go. He calculated that by driving at the enforced speed limit it would take about eight hours to get to the hotel; including a few additional stops for gas and something to eat, he would arrive around midnight. He leaned forward and turned on the radio. The knob felt loose as he twisted it to the left and then back to the right. He pushed a few buttons until he decided each station offered little; it was all too mundane. Matilda was able to ignore the radio, but he found the distraction either a comfort or an irritant. Presently, it was the latter. He needed time to think.

"Human pandemics result when a new type of virus emerges with the capacity to efficiently infect and spread. These new subtypes can develop in one of two ways." The scientist gripped the steering wheel hard as he no longer could afford to dismiss his conclusions. He ruminated, giving way to his now legitimate cause for concern. *"When an animal is infected with two different strains at the same time, the genetic material of the viruses may mix to produce a new strain containing some of the characteristics of both."* Kamer gazed with horror as he petitioned the alternative development to the forefront of his mind. *"When a virus undergoes gradual mutation it inherits the capability to infect a completely different animal species."* The voice in his head was woefully pessimistic and as the disappointed narrator recognized his fate like a fisherman in a leaky dinghy, he confessed his misgivings. *"As the result of these findings and the reevaluation of the original data, more studies are needed to conclusively prove the safety of my vaccine."*

The tired man stared out towards the darkening horizon. His foot lay heavily upon the accelerator pedal. The hum of the motor stirred within the car like the buzzing of cicadas in a summer evening. The lights ahead were dim and yellow. The lonely road and the slate sky meshed into one. Only the headlights seemed alive; everything else remained dull, banal, and ashen. His leg tingled with the sensation of falling asleep. He pushed down more heavily against the pedal and the car obeyed. The engine was no longer humming but rather chanting a hymn-like dirge that was stuck on one note. His grip on the wheel tightened as he steered into the muted and interminable night. There was no distinction between road and sky. Only the glimmer from the multiplying stars mapped the way forward. In the distance there approached a black serpent with two yellow eyes. Gradually it grew, eyes bulging, encapsulating the entire road with its blinding light. Kamer shifted forward, keeping his foot steady, steady upon the pedal; the hymn from the motor was louder, growing more intense with each vibration. "What did we do?" His daydream struggled with the release of images; his dead wife, the buried glassware, the recently deceased, and the yellow dog. They were all with him, strangely calm and quiet, all of them. He blinked them away, but only the dog remained behind. Its yellow fur muddied from the unearthing of his work. "Matilda, what's beyond the stars?" he asked. He listened for her whisper and acknowledged her silence. "That damn dog!" he cried as he steered the car straight for the oncoming headlights.

———

The gray man was beholden to no one; he was a man who didn't like sentiment and didn't like many people. He kept his memories to himself and discarded any that troubled him. The only youthful memory he could vividly recall was during late spring, right after he had turned eleven. It was the time in his life when a kind of fog had developed in his brain, a hazy mist that clogs all good senses and allows an adolescent stupor to takeover.

Myrtle Sue Crothers was his math teacher, a tall statured woman that spoke in a slow matter-of-fact manner, always referring to herself as Miss Crothers rather than using "I" in conversation. She would say things like: "Miss Crothers is going to show you how to divide," or "Miss Crothers would like you to sit down." She wore immaculately ironed clothes with stiff collars and pleated skirts, a testimony to her general pungent aroma of bleach. She maintained a carefully orchestrated classroom with strict disciplinary order that she consistently referred to. She was not disliked nor liked, she was simply tolerated. Choices she offered were clearly defined; assignments and rules were expected to be followed and those who chose not to would be dealt with according to the degree of infraction committed. The teacher never administered her own punishments, but rather referred all disciplinary actions to Mr. Sanders, a brutish and intimidating man that towered well above the tallest of children, nicknamed "the punisher".

A spindly oak desk, too small even for the prim teacher, defined the classroom. It teetered on thin legs like a well-fed heron and housed two large drawers. One exclusively for pencils, pens, erasers, and paper, while the other was reserved for confiscated items such as rubber bands, hand-balls, notes, comic books, and chewing gum. However, it was the newly added contents of the first drawer that claimed distinction among the gray man's peers, a very dead cat.

Although believed to have nine lives, this cat either did not or perhaps had used up its allotment and having been run-over just a few hours into the morning; Mrs. Wren's stripped tabby laid flat upon the dirt road. And inasmuch as its owner did not miss the poor feline at first, for it had a propensity to stray away for days at a time, two boys walking to school just happened to come across it. And what a wonderful find it was! It had been a clean bloodless kill allowing the lifeless animal to fit between two schoolbooks quite nicely, except for the paws and tail that wanted to stick out. The younger boy, however, proved quite adept at hiding the appendages under his coat as they continued their walk.

It was on their morning's journey to school that a most daring act of surprise was hatched. Taking advantage of the early hour, the culprits managed to slip the cat into the drawer of the oak desk without notice. For several hours the feline remained undetected, since there was no reason for it to be disturbed. However, after lunch, directly before arithmetic, Miss Crothers slid open the drawer to retrieve a ruler, and while reaching her hand into the opening, she unintentionally disturbed several sheets of papers exposing the grizzly carcass. Such a cruel hoax had been played upon the schoolteacher that the howl she surrendered displaced all tranquility she had finally established in her classroom.

It took just a small bit of interrogation and a handful of tattle-telling to discover the perpetrators. And though they never confessed, the two were marched into the office of "the punisher". But unlike many misdeeds before, this was not an ordinary schoolboy trick. This had been a prank of enormous magnitude; a rite of passage into adolescence. Unprovoked by Miss Crothers's demands, Mr. Sanders rediscovered a part of his own youth within this rebellious act and chose to celebrate the occasion by not dolling out his usual paddling. Standing the two boys together, he held the corpse before them with outstretched arms and then ceremoniously lowered it to his desk. And there it was, staring wide-eyed and very dead; its furry body growing stiffer with each passing tick of the wall clock.

Mr. Sanders's hands rested upon the pair of shivering shoulders, and he sighed. There was an exchange of bewildered glances between the two boys, but neither moved. They remained resolutely still for what seemed to be an interminable amount of time until "the punisher" broke the silence. "You know," he said in a deliberately quiet voice, so low that they had to strain to hear. "This was not a very smart thing to do." He cleared his throat and then did a most unlikely thing. He picked up the pencil from his desk and poked the dead cat. Both boys cringed as if the act were going to reanimate the poor creature. "I imagine though, it took a lot of nerve," he paused and cleared his throat again, "to pick it up, that is. I don't suppose you have any good plans for it now, seeing as the resting place you picked for the beast was certainly not the best choice?" Neither student moved, keeping as still as if they had lost all life, until they were suddenly reincarnated by the clamorous cry of the school bell which rang out as if it was the tolling of church bells. But rather than summoning despair, its ring created an understated alliance binding the students, the cat, and the man in a most unusual way. Nothing more was needed to be said, and by the end of the school day the dead cat had been discretely delivered to Mrs. Wren's front porch.

Twenty-Two

THE DUMP, KAMER, AND DOCTOR HOBART

The plain town's dump was open to the public from sunrise to sunset every day except Christmas, Thanksgiving, the Fourth of July, and Easter. It was not visible from the road for it had been erected behind a hillside of thorny briers and brush that had tangled among themselves, growing thick and tall over the years. A rather worn sign which read, *Town Dump*, announced its entrance. But this was a bit misleading for one had to follow a narrowing side-road for about a mile before reaching a vast wasteland of trash. At the end of the dirt road, behind a wire fence and hinged gate, sat a rickety one-room building, or as the townspeople called it, Mr. Ted's office. A rather disenchanting fellow, Ted Palling was the caretaker. And though he was not officially employed by the plain town, he was given a goodwill stipend for his troubles with free rein to take what others discarded. An unkempt and shabby looking man, he was in reality a man of unusual means, for being a Palling he was never without.

By sunrise he arrived and by sunset he departed, and except for a constant circle of vultures overhead and an occasional truck, he was always quite alone with his thoughts. His knowledge of local history was unprecedented, but since no one asked he kept his information to himself. He spoke very little and when he did, he would begin with a very long pause, so long that the listener was sure he had clearly forgotten his words. Most believed he was a dull and ignorant man, but in fact he was quite the opposite and found others to be exceptionally insipid. Rather than conversing, he chose simply to ignore and refrain from any unnecessary interactions. His only companion was a small fat cat he named Ben that fed off the mice and rats it caught.

The gray man liked Ted Palling and so he walked from the plain town to the dump. Dusty and tired he arrived, finding the cat sprawled out on the folding chair. A cup of black coffee and a half-eaten doughnut was on the workbench beside a yellow pad and broken pencil. The gray man lifted the pad and skimmed the blank pages. Only the last sheet had a listing, a telephone number that had faded with time. Shoved against the wall in a sizable box was the "catch of the day"; pieces of scrap iron and tin, a bicycle wheel with twisted spokes, and a slightly dented brass saxophone. Hanging from an over-ambitious nail was a framed reproduction of *The Mona Lisa*, a testament to the man's sense of fine art.

The sleeping cat, dripping off the seat, woke up and cast an inconsiderate glance the stranger's way and then folded its paws, tucked its head between them, and commenced to fall back to sleep. The gray man scowled and pushed the cat from the seat. It howled as it landed on its feet and quickly scampered out the open doorway. "Stupid animal," he thought, and then sat down in the chair. In front of the desk were two filthy windows. He leaned forward and peered out. In the near distance he could see the outline of Ted Palling strolling slowly toward the shack. He was rolling a wheelbarrow that tipped and rocked with the same magnitude of an ungainly skiff in rough water. The gray man got up and stood in the doorway.

"Haven't seen you around, bin' a while," the caretaker said as he rolled the wheelbarrow towards the shanty.

"Lookin' for my dog." The gray man stepped outside to greet him.

"Dog?" The wheelbarrow dropped heavily as he let go of the handles, rattling the contents of a box of somebody else's castoff junk.

"Misplaced my dog."

The other man expelled a grunt.

"Don't suppose it's been around?"

"No, no dog. "He looked up and scratched his chin. "No, just me and Ben. Coffee?"

The gray man shook his head "no" and then wandered over to the wheelbarrow. "Glass, kind of strange find."

"Couple months back, Kamer, you know that fellah that lives on the hill. Found him here pouring out liquid. I told him this was no 'dump'."

The gray man looked up and laughed.

"Sure it's a dump, but I don't allow dumpin' liquid, strictly trash and junk. If he wants to get rid of liquid I told 'em he can take it over to the river like the rest of the folks. He didn't like what I said and got mad. We got into it and the next thing I knew he was drivin' away. Anyway, today I found these still in the box; guess he fergot to take 'em." He held up an opaque flask.

The interested man reached for a corked test tube and shook it. A trace of yellow liquid trickled back down the side of the glass.

"I figure I could sell 'em; unusual for around here."

The visitor agreed, but silently wondered who might want to buy them, however, decided not to ask. "So, no dog?"

But by now Ted had answered all the questions he wanted and turned into the shack leaving the gray man standing by the wheelbarrow.

Ribbons of sunlight scattered behind a cloud and a breeze drew a warm breath and exhaled upon the earth. The vultures circled overhead forming a black halo. He gazed out into the dump and saw the cat tip-toeing over a mound of debris. Then it disappeared behind the rubbish piles. "See ya, Ted."

The impervious caretaker waved without looking up; rather, he pilfered through the ashtray, dusting off a half-smoked cigar. He lingered by the open door striking the match and puffed heartily until the smutty end glistened red. The whole of the doorframe bore the richness of his character as if it were around a museum painting instead of a rickety entranceway. The shuffle of the visitor's footsteps slowly followed the winding road, and he listened until it disappeared as silence.

———

Traveling to an out-of-the-ordinary destination is often considered a welcome distraction regardless of its distance. However, returning along the same road can be less than enjoyable. So was the walk that the gray man encountered on his way home. It was a dusty day and his mouth was dry and his mind could focus on only one thing, a cold beer. He trudged wearily, disgusted by his allegiance to the dog, chastising himself for caring. He stopped along the side of the road and put out his thumb. He felt like a vagrant; the sun was merciless and no amount of swearing could console his disgust. The plain town was not too far, but now the prospect of admitting he had walked so many miles for the dog was wearing upon his pride. The road seemed to waver under the heat as invisible flames rose and fell. He leaned into the road and waited. A truck passed in the opposite direction and tooted its horn in solidarity. Finally, in the distance he saw a car, a two-tone Chrysler with an oversized chrome bumper. It slowed down. The driver leaned over and rolled down the window. "Ride, Skipper?"

He hated nicknames, but Skipper? He couldn't imagine where the hell that came from. The gray man said, "Thanks," pulled open the door, and jumped in. A young man sporting an expertly barbered goatee turned the radio down, offered him a Lucky Strike, and then sped away leaving behind a gritty billow of road debris. He didn't care where the driver was headed as long as it passed the bar.

———

The Rosewater house was boarded up with a newly commissioned *FOR SALE* sign posted in the middle of the front yard. It was a sad looking site, and though it had always been well-groomed, weeds now prospered where grass once grew. Time was limping by and there were still no inquiries about the property. Gossip prevented any interest, which was fueled by the mysterious cause of death; all raising too many unanswered questions. Whispers ignited by the neighbors suggested that the ghosts of the three children haunted the house. The yellow dog, however, did not seem troubled by its vacancy or the prospect of ghosts, and found the neglected building more than accommodating since discovering a breach between two boards that had not been secured.

The house had become a most obliging place of refuge, especially the basement. This was where Mrs. Rosewater stored dried beef, sausage links, and canned peaches. It was cool and dry, and for the past week the dog slipped in and out as freely as if it were the owner. It liked to sit by the window and watch the road. Sometimes a car would slow down, stop, and then move on. Sometimes a child would be dared to run up to the front porch to ring the doorbell. A slight short ring was pecked and followed by the hurried scamper of feet darting away. The dog didn't care, and when the rain pounded the pane and smeared the glass with mud-stained water, it slept very well.

———

The gray man stepped out of the car. He invited the driver to join him for a drink, but was quite pleased when his invitation was declined. The Chrysler glided out of the parking lot and he watched as it faded down the chalky road. He wondered what it must be like to own such a fancy car. He looked at his watch. It was a few minutes after 4:00 p.m.; most people would still be at work. He dug into his front pocket and felt some loose change and a few bills. Two cars were parked by the door; none were familiar. He would have the place to himself. He couldn't decide if this was a good or bad thing.

The entrance door had recently been painted red, and he frowned noting the color was changed from black. Apparently the clean-up was not complete since several strips of tape still covered the handle. Without any thought, he grabbed hold making the grim discovery it was sticky, as though some of the adhesive had bled through. "Shit," he thought as he wiped his hand on his pants. Cursing the handle again, he pulled the door open but this time using only the crook of his index and middle finger. The smell of cigarette smoke and old beer broke free. The air conditioner wedged in the back window with rolled newspaper to keep the flies out rattled noisily reminding him to enter quickly and shut the door. This was one of the few places where you could escape the heat without paying admission.

He glanced about and then settled upon the first stool. He peered over the counter for the bartender. He waited for a moment and twisted round in his seat. Two men were sitting at a back table. Several empty beer mugs and a bowl of peanuts took up most of the tabletop, while the full mugs were confined within the circle of their stooped postures. They nodded their heads in agreeable camaraderie, yet only the lean fellow talked boisterously while the barracuda faced man moved his jaw nervously as if rolling his tongue over the words that were lining up in his mouth as he listened.

"What's yer pleasure, Bud?"

The gray man turned back towards the bartender who had appeared as if he had just materialized out of thin air. "Beer, on tap." How he hated to be called Bud.

"Beer on tap." The request was repeated as the bartender shuffled over to the center of the bar.

The gray man slid a half-filled bowl of salted peanuts in front of him. He leaned over and began to pick through the remains. "Don't like the dark ones," he explained.

The bartender set the glass mug before him and nodded. "Never liked burnt ones, either. But a boiled peanut, now that's something to really hate. Ever eat one?"

The gray man shook his head, "Can't stand them things, too damn mushy."

"Yea, mushy. You're right!" He reached down under the bar and retrieved the burlap sack. Today his generosity filled the bowl to the brim.

The thirsty patron slurped his beer and then wiped the froth-moustache from his upper lip. "Seen Gil Adler around? He's usually in here, no matter what time of the day."

"Adler," there was a momentary pause. "Come to think of it, I ain't seen him around lately. You're right."

Both men shook their heads as if contemplating the missing man's whereabouts. "Maybe he's sick."

"Maybe." But this admission did not seem to stir much more concern. The gray man poked about the bowl and then looked up. "Don't suppose you've seen a dog around here?"

"Seen a cat; out by the alley. Kind of beat up looking thing; like it'd been in a fight, but no dog. A while ago maybe, but not recently. What color was it?"

"Yellow."

"Yellow? I've seen a tan dog before, but can't say I've ever seen a yellow one. Are ya sure it's yellow?"

"Course I'm sure, it's my dog."

"What happened? Ya loose it?"

The owner scowled with the accusation that he had lost his dog. "No, it just left."

"Why?"

"I don't know why. 'Cause it's a dog. They do shit like that."

"And that's why I don't have a dog or a wife. They have a tendency to run off." The bartender smiled. "Another brew?"

"Sure," the gray man said without hesitation. "One for the road."

The rain was indifferent. It fell without wind and beaded the road with drops that rolled, clinging one to the other until the entire pavement was a clear glaze of water. The land soaked up the rain and was transformed from deep ochre to a rich brown; dirt that once flaked and dusted the road became sticky and as it rained the earth smelled more alive.

The gray man jogged down the sidewalk and his legs moved with a speed that he had not remembered before. Water dripped from his hair down to his face and neck, and his wet shirt and pants stuck to his skin. His feet slapped the road tossing more water from the puddles onto his shoes and socks, and he kept running. A sense of well-being washed over him. The dog wagged its tail as the man jogged past the Rosewater's front window. The blinds had been drawn shut, yet were raised just above the sill allowing enough of a vantage point to see the comings and goings outside. The gray man did not slow down but continued to flee along the street as if being chased, and the dog thumped its tail happily with the brief encounter with his master. It watched for a little longer and then, as rain often does to the weary, it closed its eyes and fell asleep.

Midnight came and went and the rain continued to fall. The storm tore at the trees. Like the crack of a homerun bat a limb broke away from its constellation of branches. It woke the dog out of its sleep. Hungry, it got up and slinked down the basement stairs. The wooden planks wobbled as it skulked into the lightless chamber and damp brown air. Only a splinter of moonlight had smuggled its way in through the thin window, leading with an anemic beam like arteries belonging to the rusting furnace. The hound sniffed the air and then scavenged about the floor, but did not find anything to eat for he had already consumed all the dried beef and sausages that had been stored. Only the peaches remained on the shelf in jars marked Peaches with the date they had been preserved.

The dog chased the moonbeam to the furnace and barked at it angrily. It lowered itself before the giant and growled fiercely. But the furnace did not respond and remained steadfast. The dog snarled again, barring its teeth; however, soon found little reason

to continue its threat and scampered back up the steps of the cata-
comb and hid beneath the stairwell.

When the rain stopped the house grew quiet and woke the
dog. It crept out from under the stairwell and stood up. It brought
its legs forward, stretched, yawned, and lumbered over to the window. It was still dark outside and except for the porch light belonging to the house across the street, the world remained in a
haze of sleep. The dog sat looking out the streaked window. Drips
fell from the gutter and occasionally were blown onto the window.
The dog licked the window as the drops slid down the glass, teasing the canine with its veins of water crisscrossing the pane. The
dog was thirsty so it got up and snuck back outside between the
boards and followed the night in search of water.

———

He was blinded by dawn; its orange and pink bands flooded the
horizon, dripping over and saturating the landscape like a spilled
summer drink. Kamer rolled over onto his side. Beneath him was
a coarse bed of gravel and pebbles. He only vaguely remembered
how he had gotten there; the swerving off the road and the near-
miss. He listened. There beside him was the inhaling and exhaling
of rapid breathing. He extended his fingers. He wanted to reach
up and touch it, but his arms were too heavy. He lifted his head
and squinted, filtering the light. A yellow image was trotting away
towards the sunlight. He lay his head down and turned his face.
A drizzle of thoughts sprinkled over him and then like a colos-
sal shower realization rained down with a loneliness like no other.
There was no shelter that could shield him from such a storm.
He looked back towards the rising sun. The clarity of the night

mingled about his brain as he pulled himself up. His car was parked headfirst in the field and appeared undamaged. He rubbed the back of his neck and found enough strength to stand. His legs wobbled as if he had been out at sea and as he took a step, he leaned forward, bending over with new found grief. "Damn," he said and put his hands in his pocket. His keys were not there. He stumbled over to the car and opened the door. His briefcase was sitting on the front seat as if it were a passenger waiting to say, "I told you so."

He sank down behind the wheel and found the key already in the ignition. He looked at his hand, poised ready to start the car when the strength of his glance suddenly interrupted the turning of the key. "Shit," he muttered. A cold fringe of sweat formed above his brow. He rubbed his hands against his shirt and a rush of nausea welled up inside. "Shit!" he exclaimed. "Shit! It's the dog!"

———

Dr. Hobart rested his head against the back of the chair, a position already taken up by the shadow of the floor lamp. Its granite hue fell over his face which added a bit more melancholy to his already grim expression. His office, a room that once seemed to him such an important place, now made him feel depressed. He slid a cigarette out of the pack and tapped the end against the desk. He had quit smoking, but today his good intentions were set aside. The coroner reports were stacked before him in four distinct piles. He set his pad alongside of the papers. "Where is that lighter?" he grumbled. He pulled open the top drawer and slid the pencils and papers aside. But the only thing he retrieved was his misplaced letter opener.

The cigarette mocked him as he feverishly hunted the other drawers, ransacking what was once an array of tidily arranged items. A worn book of matches with barely enough strike-surface had been tossed to the back of the bottom drawer along with a cardboard box of birthday candles. He smiled, pitched the candles aside, and lit a match. It quivered meekly. He cupped his hands around the stick as if all mankind depended upon this pathetic flame and drew in on the filter. The cigarette ignited. He flicked the match out and then coughed like a teenager with his first butt. His eyes stung as the smoke drifted into his face, and he wondered why he was smoking. But after several deep inhales he remembered, and the exaggerated drags seemed to calm his shattered nerves as he sank into solemn thought

Tissue samples from the autopsies had been examined by four individual labs in four different locations. Only someone like himself who had correlated the information would have concluded that all of the deceased had been infected by the same virus.

Someone sneezed. He looked down at his watch noting the timely arrival of the cleaning woman. He envisioned her dumping the wastebasket into a larger receptacle and then brushing her hands over her faded-blue smock. A soft patter of feet shuffled across the floor, and then they stopped. If the office door was closed it was a signal that he was too busy to be disturbed. He stared at the knob waiting for it to turn; but heard only the soft shuffle of shoes padding away. He was pleased. He didn't feel like a lecture about smoking.

The doctor took another long drag from the cigarette, exhaled slowly, and then crushed it out in his saucer as if ungrateful for the small moment of pleasure it had provided. An unpleasant smell of tobacco stained his fingers. He dumped the butt and ashes into the wastebasket and tossed the pack into the top drawer. He leaned back into a sullen silence and gave himself to deep thought like a benediction.

Any exchange of body fluids, such as saliva through a bite, would easily transmit the virus to a new host. None of the deceased had any contact with each other nor were any puncture wounds found. He pulled the pad towards him and scanned his notes. *The incubation period had not been officially determined, but by all his gatherings the mutated virus was able to infect a new individual in a fairly short amount of time; perhaps as little as a few days.* The names of the deceased were even more familiar in his own handwriting. He had known them all, yet had very little information to draw upon. Each name came with a personal recognition, and he slid his finger across the pad like one strokes a face.

He pushed himself away from the desk and stood over his papers contemplating certain basic facts. *A virus can enter the human body with the single act of rubbing one's eyes or nose. Therefore, transmission did not have to occur by way of a bite. In effect, it was also quite probable that the carrier was not necessarily a feral animal, but very possibly a domesticated one.*

Turning towards the window, he pulled the curtain aside. *Sid Calhoun, the Rosewater children, and the two women; the timing of their deaths are too coincidental not to be connected, and then there was the young waitress and Doug Fairbanks.* Several cars drove past and splashed water from a large and almost impassable puddle up onto the sidewalk. He had an urge for another cigarette, but the stink from his hands suggested otherwise. He walked into the small office bathroom and turned on the tap to wash them. A pressed linen cloth was draped over the towel rack. It looked proportionally flimsy in contrast to the thick brass rod it was hung upon. He looked into the rectangular mirror over the sink as he dried his hands and then put his palm up to his nose. It smelled medicinal, a good smell for a doctor. He leaned forward and opened his mouth; the small lump in his throat now appeared redder and more inflamed. He pulled down his lower eyelid and examined his pupil; then the other.

All silent recollections of the past month suddenly were compacted into that single rainy afternoon when he picked up a hitchhiker, brought it home, and fed it dinner. He stared wide-eyed into the mirror at his crumbling appearance pressed against the stiffly starched collar. He turned the faucet on again, but this time scrubbed his hands harshly with the brown soap. "Idiot!" he hollered. "Damn, idiot! And you call yourself a doctor!" But the terror behind the anxious expression looking back only responded with a pitiful quiver of despair. He quickly turned out of the bathroom, but not before flinging the cloth and soap into the wastebasket.

He spun the desk chair round and threw himself into the seat. The forecast for the future was veiled in gloom. He swallowed and acknowledged the lump in his throat ever more present; as if it had grown larger in the short time he had walked from the bathroom to his desk. He slid the pad towards him and added another column to the list of names. Then he penciled in "Hobart". He flipped back to a previous sheet and beneath the word "host" he scribbled one word, "dog". Putting his head in his hands, he simply moaned.

Twenty-Three

THE RAIN AND A CAR RIDE

There is a welcome solitude in rain. Only once in the history of the plain town was there a time when rain was scarce. This was the year the earth became parched and dry and crumbled into a fine powder that covered the land and the houses and the wagons. What was once green turned brown. The sun scorched and withered anything that dared to grow. It was a time when the cows grew thin and gaunt like the people. There was little to eat and what was tilled in the spring had been put up the summer before. When the winds blew the dust and dirt sandblasted the town, and it choked the throats and pricked the skin, so no one talked or ventured outdoors. This was a long time ago when the plain town became silent.

———

The rain was lashing at the gray man's window, and he stopped packing to look outside. In the fields the wind was rolling and tossing waves of grass, while beyond the horizon the wheat, tall and slender, was bowing beneath its own weight, quivering under the storm's mutiny. A harshness swept across the afternoon sky as lightening flashed, colliding with the madness of splitting and severing land. Water was bleeding into the fissures and fractures and crevices and was siphoned by tendrils belonging to the rooted plants.

But the plain town tames the rains and when it rolls down the roof, it captures it in tin gutters. Like a fast moving stream, the water follows the path downward, plunging along the side of the buildings and into the streets where it diverts left and right and forward. Some water slides into oily puddles beside and under parked cars where it waits for the sun to make a gasoline rainbow.

The knapsack lay open on his bed next to a heap of clean clothes. He picked through the pile, rolling them up and arranging them evenly across the bottom. He knew he was a lousy packer, but this was the only way he could get everything to fit. His clothes were laid out like his emotions, and he would keep them coiled tightly until needed. To unfold your feelings is to just ask for disappointment. He had stashed a hundred dollars in the dresser. He rummaged about the drawer and pulled out a single brown sock. He wriggled his hand into the neck and then as though putting them on, extended his reach and fingered the bill. He unraveled his hand and rolled the sock into a ball. He shifted the packed clothes and sandwiched it between his shirts.

The rain continued to drum; shattering like glass bubbles, forming puddles, and then spilling out into any open space, pillaging the land with mud. He folded over the flap and fumbled with the buckles. These had given him trouble the last time he took a trip. After two tries and an expletive of "go in you mother!" the stubborn one surrendered. He moved the canvas to the floor and then lay down. He closed his eyes. The weary man took inventory as he mentally searched the station wagon. He had put his poles and tackle box across the rear seats. His rubber boots; he had to think a moment before remembering they were stowed beneath the tarp on the floor. He couldn't recall if he had rinsed off the muck from the last time he wore them. But he would have smelled them by now if he hadn't.

A year had passed since he and the dog went fishing. *It had been a remarkably hazy day. In the quiet of that morning the breeze brushed against the leaves, turning out the harmony of a wind harp. The fog was ascending from the water like meringue and the greatness of the lake could only be imagined for it lay camouflaged under a blanket of mist. The surface split beneath the weathered planks as dog, man, and boat drifted carelessly with the idle current. He had cast his hook into the pale oatmeal sky and when it dropped it splashed and startled the quiet. The line rose and grew slack. He leaned forward, resting the pole against his leg, and the dog stared out. The sun refused to show itself, concealing its presence between veils of slate clouds. A misty rain sprinkled upon the lake and dimpled the slick surface. From beneath the water the fish interpreted this as an illusion of water bugs and came up to be fed. "Should 'av brought a net," he thought. The yellow dog stretched its neck over the side and tried to lap the water with its tongue. He set the pole down and dumped out the minnows and scooped some lake water into the bait pail. But the dog wasn't interested in the pail and leaned its head over the side again.*

As the fog disappeared it exposed a strand of trees standing like misplaced furniture in the middle of the cove. The dog was patient, but at the end of the day when they rowed to shore, it jumped out of the boat and ran up and down the shoreline until it lost interest and rested in the shade beside the station wagon. In the summers, when the man was a small boy, he would take a jar and net and walk along the shore. He followed the line of weed-beds growing in the mire or followed the break-line up and around thorny rocks. By the end of the day he would return with a jar full of tadpoles that his mother would make him spill back into the lake.

He shifted the pile of unpacked clothes with his leg and stretched out. He listened to the rain and wondered where the dog was now. He would leave when the rain stopped.

———

Kamer parked the car by the side of the house and watched as the storm tore at the clouds as easily as if lifting the edges of paper. Seeing no signs of clearing, he made a dash for the front porch. All good intentions of keeping dry had been foiled. Washed by the rain his white hair dripped into his eyes and down his back. A cool gust of wind like an unexpected visitor blew over him. He shivered like a wet animal and leaned into the door. His fingers fumbled with the ring of keys, finally releasing the lock. However, when he tried to take a step forward his shoe was fused to the floor. A sticky film of mud had adhered to the soles like tar. Weary with disgust at having muddied his newly polished oxfords, they were promptly slipped off and set aside. He stood on the door mat in his stocking feet; another mismatched pair, one black and one navy. He defended the error with a plausible excuse that the colors were equally dark enough for anyone to have mistaken the two as an exact pair. Returning to the lock, he turned the key again and pushed against the door. The wind conspired against him and blew across the porch, tossing his shoes into the rain. They rolled off the deck and down into the rose bed. A momentary thought of retrieving them crossed his mind, however, the welcome solitude of the house quickly overcame any act of heroism, and he stepped inside and quickly shut out the rain.

———

In the morning the white house on the top of the hill began to dry out. The sun filtered into the bedroom by way of a split in the curtains. A stream of daylight had wandered in and now presented itself as a sampling of the day to be. Proud and brilliant it drew a yellow line down the dresser to the floor and spread itself over the coiled rug like spilled honey. The walls began to creak while warming in the morning sun. Water slipped off the overhanging branches, hitting the roof with an occasional ping. A mockingbird pecked the tin gutter as it gleaned a drink from the trough. Kamer lay in bed awake and deciphered the noises of the house. The refrigerator was humming, reminding him that it was time to defrost the freezer. He stretched and slid out from under his quilt. The floorboards ached as he stepped across the room. He poured a pitcher full of water into the porcelain basin and then leaned forward to splash tepid water on his face. This was a luxury dating back to his childhood. And though he had indoor plumbing put in years ago; he still enjoyed this old-fashioned ritual.

The house often spoke to him. On cold nights the furnace would complain, sometimes spitting, sometimes groaning. In the summertime the pipes would whistle whenever he ran the hot water. In the wintertime the roof would pop. He understood the house's language. But this morning he wished it would leave him alone because he was listening; listening for the return of the yellow dog.

For a long time there was no bridge over the river and only when the water was low could people get their wagons across. Finally, a low-water bridge was built near the mouth, but those folks who lived far away still had to count on the goodness of Mother Nature or go around for several extra miles.

———

The plain town awoke to broken light and dampness shedding its morning gray with remnants of a leftover rainbow. It wasn't until you drove through Main Street and followed the road out of town that the world changed from white to green. But there was always a dependable trail of brown leading in and out of town; sometimes in the form of dust and other times in the form of mud. This morning it was mud that assailed the gray man's vehicle; adhering to the tires as he rumbled along, splattering the rims and speckling the doors. He grumbled every time he dipped down into a pothole, cementing his displeasure with the overuse of the roads.

He leaned his elbow on the open window's ledge, steering the station wagon with a degree of unfamiliar contentment and reviewed his agenda. He grinned with the prospect of fishing. It was not an act that he often did, grinning with pleasure, yet if ever there was a time that afforded such an expression of satisfaction, this was it. Sunlight was warming the land and as he drove he broke the silence. The engine sputtered and hiccupped, and he was pleased because he was alone. Sharing space, even if it was on the lake as vast and secluded as the one he fished, was an intrusion. He had no problem with people, it was just that he needed his own piece of the earth; a destination he could return to and find that the only disturbance was made by nature herself. City folks didn't understand the immersion of self with nature, nor did they contemplate times of day with the same sensitivity. In the plain town you didn't require a clock to tell what time it was. Mornings arrived with a pot of coffee. Midday was summoned by the arrival of mail, and afternoons concluded with mothers calling children in for supper. But once you got outside of the plain town, time was revealed by looking up. The complexion of the sky portrayed each of the 24 hours, all in various shades and mixtures of the primary colors. The later the day the richer the color until it turned to ebony and then lightened again until dawn. Then the color wheel would rotate with the earth and start all over again.

The gray man turned on the wipers and they slapped away the mist streaking the dirty windshield. As if turning the surrounding landscape into a sepia toned photograph, he bemoaned his decision and pulled over to the side of the road to clean the glass. Morning calls that were usually muffled or extinguished by the passing cars and trucks along the road beckoned him to turn off the motor. He stepped out of the car and breathed deeply. The fields resounded with the rally of birds and insects, and unnamed rustling. He leaned back into the station wagon and then reached behind the seat for the rag. He balled it up and wiped the outside of the window. At first he only managed to smear the mud around, but finally after several more attempts, he was able to secure a clean surface. He tossed the rag behind the seat. Streams of light angled off the windshield and ricocheted back to the ground. Generally the field looked as though it was comprised of a single sheet of green felt, but now, the dew captured the sunlight and glazed each shaft as if they were blades of steel. He shielded his eyes and turned his look towards the road. In the near distance he could make out a silhouette trailing the wavy outline. The road dipped up and down and he lost sight of the figure behind the rise. The stillness of the air was disturbed by a sudden breeze, and it roused the gnats and courted him back into the car. Would the image reappear like the early light edging slowly upward from beneath the horizon?

Turning his gaze back to the dashboard, he became conscious that his thoughts had strayed. Now with little else on his mind, except for which lure he was going to use, he dismissed the image and started-up the engine. It sputtered like an old man. He gave it more gas and it finally gave in. Settling down into a noisy hum, he shifted into first and slowly prodded the old rattletrap onward. Clods of dried mud crumbled off the tires as he rumbled forward and back onto the paved road.

He was sensitive to the morning's glow and like a slow shutter admitting in light, he wondered about himself and the dog. Together they were two merely posing for a picture. The awakening day stirred as the scene before him materialized. His thoughts reacted like being snapped by a camera, within him emotions turned upside down. But now he could turn them right side up, even retouch as if burnishing a negative. He could rid his life of the canine by merely leaving it behind. This accidental meeting; this chance reunion on a common country road; he had the freedom to control how much of himself he would parcel out. He slowed the car and trolled alongside of the yellow dog. As though it were deaf to the vehicle beside it, the dog's pace was lively, and it dragged its nose along the road with the intent of finding something of interest. The gray man steered with one hand and peered down from the driver's side window and then back up to the road.

Did a special bond between himself and the dog ever exist or had he concocted this contrived platitude of "dog is man's best friend"? Perhaps the yellow dog was just another mutt like just another empty frame in the attic. It was a scruffy looking fellow, its fur matted with patches of caked mud; thinner than he remembered. He stopped driving and let the dog scamper ahead of him. It zigzagged along the edge of the road and then wandered into the medium where it was enveloped by a hazy mirage of morning light. The dog started down the rise and from where he sat he could only see the tip of the tail as it finally dipped away. A brown sedan whizzed past and raced down the hill out of view. A frantic car horn sounded and electrified the stillness of the morning. In an instant the gray man jammed down hard on the clutch and shoved the gearstick into first; it squealed in displeasure. The station wagon set itself into gear and rumbled down the incline just as the brown car was breaking across the horizon line.

"Here, boy!" his voice cracked under the strain of misunderstanding. He leaned his head out of the window, "I'm tired of chasing you!" The car idled with noisy trepidation. "Come, boy!" he shouted. His voice choked with disappointment. He wiped his sleeve across his eyes and pressed up and down upon the accelerator with the same indecisiveness as his emotions.

When nature had sovereignty its green shrubs and barbed thickets stretched and wandered with impunity. But when the tangled brush was tamed the black road was built. On either side remained the green and brown earth of planted fields. But every few miles nature reclaimed her land, and this is where the yellow dog had reemerged. It settled itself on the side of the road under the shade of the scrub brush as if it knew; knew that the gray man would return.

The station wagon pulled up, and when the yellow dog saw the gray man it stood up and wagged its tail. The owner leaned over, opened the passenger side, and tapped the seat with his hand. Immediately the dog jumped in and attacked its master with affection. It licked his face and nestled its head against his chest; all the while whimpering.

The driver laughed and pushed the dog away. "Where the hell have you been?" He gave the dog a gentle slap on its back as it stretched out to sleep. Its tail wagged vigorously, then lightly, until it was tucked snuggly around its body.

The gray man put the car into gear and started back along the road. It was a fine day to fish; a very fine day indeed. He glanced into the rearview mirror and behind him in the distance he could see rain clouds smeared across the sky like gray paint. They hovered over the plain town as if it was being stalked by a horde of ravens. He looked over at his sleeping companion. It was resting comfortably. "Damn, dog!" he thought and shook his head with a strange feeling of uncertainty.

Epilogue

Lloyd Tritch looked out across the lake where the gray man and the dog were fishing. He traced their slow monotonous drift in and out of the wine-stained shadows. A color too mournful for such a peaceful day; an observation, he noted, not to be questioned but rather to be accepted. The Preacher's compassion was as big as a European cathedral. In the summer his sermons were hot and fiery and in the winter they were as severe as the ice cracking the snow-laden branches. The plain town had never seen a man quite as sensitive and committed as the Preacher. Like a painter who seizes the canvas, so did he select his subjects that suited his moods. But in time the Preacher's palette faded, and there wasn't any more paint on the canvas.

CPSIA information can be obtained
at www.ICGtesting.com
Printed in the USA
LVOW11s1623180717
541772LV00005B/925/P